# MESMERISING SHORT STORIES

## DEEPANSHU SRIVASTAVA

ISBN
Paperback  979-8-89673-335-5
Hardcase  979-8-89777-387-9

*My Loving Mother*

*"Dedicated to my mother, my profound inspiration,*
*Ms Manju Srivastava,*
*who now lives in the stars. May these tales reach her"*

# ACKNOWLEDGEMENTS

Writing this book has been a long but pleasant process, filled with persistence and inspiration from endless reserves of my senior writers, playwrights and a number of people. My passion for reading books, watching episodic soap operas and training in screenplay writing at the prestigious FTII of Pune and Whistling Woods, Mumbai, have greatly inspired and influenced my writings. I express my wholehearted thanks to my senior storytellers, screenwriters, and the faculty at FTII and Whistling Woods for the creative spark provided by them. Most importantly, if any of my work is similar to theirs, it is purely involuntary.

I also express my gratitude to Dr. V. Nath, Ph. D., and Mr. Shri Prakash for their continued motivation throughout the preparation of this work. I would also thankfully acknowledge Professors Mayuresh Belsare, ex-HOD, and Dr. Ankit Singh, my teachers during my postgrads, for helping me build up confidence as a writer. My confidence also received a boost from the overwhelming response of the readers of my earlier book, Interesting Stories. This book owes its existence to all the above people.

The editorial team at Notion Press deserves applause for their insightful feedback and dedication to shaping the content in its nice form. Finally, a big thanks to the readers of the book who embarked on this adventure with me and for giving the characters of the twenty-five stories a home in their imaginations.

# Contents

# 1. THE WILL POWER (SPIRIT)

Somewhere, in Mumbai, Vikramjeet Bhonsale, nicknamed "Vicky", is a former Indian Air Force captain who dreams of starting a low-cost carrier airline. He idolises Mr Naresh Deshmukh, the owner of Fly High Airlines. One day, Vicky is visited by Rituja "Ritu" Patil, whose family is looking for a groom for her. Rituja is a fiery young woman who wants to open her own bakery. Vicky is impressed by Ritu's drive and agrees to marry her. He tells her that he grew up as an ambitious youth, who was ready to go to any extent to get his wishes fulfilled and his work done. Vicky had joined the Indian Air Force, where he excelled but was often reprimanded by his superior, Mr Raghvan Nair, due to his high-handedness.

Once, when his father was on his deathbed in Mumbai, Vicky was in Chennai. He tried to book a flight home to be with his father but did not have enough money. He asked several people at the Chennai airport to help him out financially but everyone looked away. After a tough and long journey by train and road, when he finally reached his house, he discovered that his father had died and his last rites were already completed. This event sparked Vicky's ambition to start a low-cost carrier airline. Ritu, however, rejects the idea of marrying him because she feels that she and Vicky are already married to their respective ambitions in their lives.

After the passing away of his father, Vicky visits Mr Raghvan Nair, asking for the ex-serviceman loan. Having quit the Indian Air Force after his father's demise, he wished to somehow start his own low-cost airline. However, Raghvan refuses. With no other option left, Vicky travels from Chennai to Mumbai. Incidentally, Mr Naresh Deshmukh is travelling on the same flight and Vicky decided to meet him. On the flight, Vicky proposes the idea of a low-cost airline to Mr Naresh, suggesting a collaboration. However, on the other hand, Naresh believes that the poor should not travel with the rich and rejects Vicky's proposal and humiliates him.

Mr Niranjan Shah, the head of a venture capital firm, also travelling on the same flight, overhears Vicky's conversation with Naresh and asks Vicky to explain his business plan to his firm's board, which is present with him on the same flight. The board likes Vicky's idea and together they strike a business plan. Vicky was on his way to making his dream come true. On the other hand, during this period, Vicky and Ritu start meeting each other frequently, getting to know each other better, and overcoming their differences. They eventually decide to get married.

To start his own low-cost airline, Vicky plans to lease a Boeing aircraft from a private aviation company, Together In The Air. The company, impressed by Vicky's dedication, ambition, and passion towards his dream, agrees to lease the aircraft to Vicky and his business partner, Niranjan. After getting his funds sanctioned, Vicky meets with the officials at the Directorate General of Civil Aviation (DGCA) to acquire the licence but this is disregarded by them. After many attempts, he is finally able to meet the President Of India and requests her help in getting the licence. With the President Of India's help, Vicky finally manages to get his much-desired licence to work towards his dream of starting a low-cost carrier airline.

Irked by the progress of Vikramjeet, Naresh uses his power to pass a law that requires the Boeing aircraft to submit its airline blueprint to be able to fly in the Indian airspace. Together In The Air cancels the lease and demands a penalty fee. Vicky requests Niranjan to lend him money to pay the penalty, but Niranjan refuses. Niranjan also reveals that he was actually working with Naresh and that he and Naresh had together conspired to bring Vicky down. He also tells Vicky that Fly High Airlines has acquired the Boeing aircraft instead. Infuriated, Vicky storms into Naresh's office, but he is tackled by the guards. This incident affects Vicky, making him short-tempered. He often quarrels with Ritu, but later apologises.

Vicky realises that he doesn't need a big aircraft. He can fly smaller aircraft which need not ally with any big name in the aviation industry. Therefore, working ahead in this direction, he struck a deal with a Turboprop aircraft manufacturer to start his own small low-cost carrier airline, which he named, "Konkan Air". On the other hand, Naresh, fearing Vicky may affect his business, decides to take the matter into his own hands. He is up to something.

Meanwhile, Vicky's entire friend circle helps him by donating as much money as they can for him to start his airlines. He plans to commence flight operations from airstrips that have been abandoned since the major airports came under Naresh's company's control. Vicky sells the tickets for his "Konkan Air" at railway stations and petrol pumps. Retired Air Force pilots are hired by Vicky to fly his aircraft, and Ritu wins the bid for the in-flight catering in Vicky's aircraft.

On the day of the delivery of the aircraft, Naresh uses his influence to restrict the flight's landing at Sahar Domestic Airport, Mumbai, forcing Vicky's flights to crash-land at

Lohegaon Air Force Station due to the lack of fuel. To this incident, Raghvanan summons Vicky to explain the emergency landings and lets Vicky off with a warning and fine. The airline's maiden flight from Mumbai, which was scheduled from Mumbai to Goa, catches fire and is forced to abort its take-off. When Vicky investigates this entire matter, he finds out that Naresh had bribed the captain of his aircraft to sabotage the flight and let the fire engulf the flight when it was mid-air.

Vicky complains about this matter to Raghavan Nair. The pilot admits his mistake in front of the enquiry panel set up by Raghavan. Mr Kunal Shinde, a Mumbai-based prominent businessman, offers to buy Konkan Air. According to Mr Shinde, Vicky is unable to handle the airline properly, and it is facing financial losses. However, Vicky denies selling his Konkan Air to Shinde.

After learning that Konkan Air is continuing despite undergoing heavy losses, Naresh starts a smear campaign against Konkan Air in the hopes of ending Vicky's dreams. However, Vicky assures everybody that his flights are safe and cost-effective through mass advertisements. When he relaunches his Konkan Air, no passengers check in for even one of the flights. He is about to give up when he is informed that a technical error resulted in no tickets being booked for that particular "first" flight, whereas all the other flights are fully booked. With tears of happiness in his eyes, Vicky watches the other flights touch down on the ground and take off. After some days, Naresh calls Vicky and offers to work with him, but Vicky rejects the offer, saying "farmers have flown and will continue to fly". He also reminds Naresh that he does not own the "sky". Naresh accepts defeat as Konkan Air becomes a success.

Konkan Air is a super-hit airline, not only in Maharashtra but also at the national level. One day, the **Civil Aviation Minister** of India summons Naresh and reprimands him for sabotaging Konkan Air's inaugural flight, and threatens to shut down Fly High Airlines.

After Naresh returns to Mumbai from New Delhi, in the restroom of Sahar Domestic Airport in Mumbai, he thinks about the entire episode of Vicky, Konkan Air, the success of Konkan Air, the Civil Aviation Minister's scolding, and his threat to shut down Fly High Airlines. Suddenly, he suffers an anxiety attack. He tries to take his pill, but it falls to the floor. A janitor working in the restroom picks up the pill for Naresh. This event changes Naresh's thought process completely. The incident induces in Naresh a sense of respect for lower-income groups and the not-so-rich people in society.

Now, it is June 2024, and Vicky and Ritu's airline, Konkan Air, is one of the top five airlines in the country. Vicky and Ritu smile as they recall how, because of Vicky's "willpower" (spirit) and Ritu's unconditional support, they have managed to fulfil their dreams and have completely transformed their lives and lives of many other people for the better.

# 2. THE FAITH

Champaklal Shah, a caterer by profession, lives in a Gujarati Hindu household in Ahmedabad with his wife and two grown children. His elder son makes him fix his engagement with a girl of their choice from a strict Hindu cult. Extremely derisive towards Muslims, he starts his days with the old songs of a Punjabi Sikh pop singer Manjeet Manchala, who has now stopped producing albums and disappeared mysteriously. He has regular arguments with a Muslim neighbour, Nawab Salman Ali.

One day, Champaklal visits his late mother's bank vault to collect her belongings. He then finds adoption papers certifying he was adopted in 1960. After glancing at all the details, he decides to get the details of his biological parents and visits the orphanage from where he was adopted. He discovers that he was born into a Muslim family. This shocks him, considering how much he dislikes Muslims, and he decides to keep this a secret. Eventually, he admits to Nawab that he is also a Muslim and that he must find his real father, Ahmadullah, and speak to him. They discover that Ahmadullah is in a critical condition due to old age and is living in a senior home. The Imam taking care of Ahmadullah tells Champaklal that if Ahmadullah saw that his only son had been brought up as a non-Muslim, it could cause severe damage to his health. Therefore, he tells Champaklal to learn how to become a true Muslim and come back to meet Ahmadullah once he is ready.

With the help of Nawab, Champaklal begins to learn the ways of Muslim people. However, the Imam declines Champaklal's request to meet Ahmadullah once again, claiming he is still not coming across as a true Muslim. Meanwhile, Champaklal's son, Akash, falls in love with a young girl named Ritika and to marry her, he must have her father accept him and his family. Ritika's father is a devout follower of a spiritual godman named Premanand. Seeking to help him impress Ritika's father, Akash asks Champaklal to also follow Premanand and become spiritual. However, on one occasion, Champaklal ends up admitting publicly that he is a born Muslim. Champaklal's family and Ritika's father witness this, and Premanand advises Ritika's father not to have Ritika marry Akash. Due to this, Champaklal's family leaves him. A case is lodged against Champaklal for offending Muslims, and in court, the Imam serves as a character witness of how Champaklal detests Islam. His witness backfires when Nawab, now Champaklal's attorney, accuses the Imam of trying to wrongfully convert Champaklal to Islam.

The court permits Champaklal to see an ailing Ahmadullah. However, before they arrive at the senior home, Ahmadullah has already died. Furious over the whole situation, Champaklal tries to bring down Premanand, the main cause of most of his troubles. He then accidentally discovers that Premanand's eye twitches due to a very rare abnormality causing contraction of the eyelid, which Manchala also suffered from. This reminds Champaklal that Manchala had disappeared years ago, and then matches the voices of Manchala and Premanand, confirming they are the same person. He then crashes an event of Premanand and reveals to a large audience how Premanand is actually a Sikh and has been a fraud and characterless pop singer with various cases lodged against him for adulterous relationships with many women. He gives a speech on how the religion a person follows should not matter as long as they are acting rightfully. Champaklal's family finally returns to him, and Akash is allowed to marry Ritika.

# 3. THE ARTIST

This story is a tragedy about a veteran theatre actor Bhalerao, also known as Appa, who was an acclaimed theatre actor during his days. He garnered fame and fortune by acting in plays based on various literary works, especially those of **William Shakespeare**. He wins the award and the highest title of *Rangmanch Ka Shahenshah*. Subsequently, Appa bequeaths all of his wealth to his children.

Appa never keeps anything to himself and expresses his views very frankly, not hesitating to use expletives while expressing his views. Only his wife Vasundhara, whom he fondly calls 'Sarkar', and his close friend Gangadhar can understand his nature. His daughter-in-law Dimple and son Omkar could not appreciate his frank nature, which at times led to embarrassing situations when they have visitors or when their daughter hurls expletives at school.

The breaking point in their relationship comes when their granddaughter performs a folk dance taught by Appa, which is not appreciated by her mother Dimple. An argument ensues between them and when they return home, Dimple slaps her daughter. The next day, Dimple proposes to part ways with them by moving out, a ploy through which she anticipates that Appa will grant them their space. Appa sees through her plan and decides to move out while remarking to his son, "The whole world is a stage, and unfortunately, my part is a sad one."

Appa's wife, Vasundhara, is very devoted to him and she does not question his decisions. They move to their son-in-law and daughter Pooja's place. Appa continues with his carefree and frank ways, at times laden with a few expletives. Their son-in-law, Pranav, is a high-ranking engineer in his company and is caring. Pooja also confronts similar embarrassing situations as Dimple, but her husband, Pranav, does not seem to mind it. He appreciates Appa's fluent style of recitals. On Pooja's anniversary, when they had invited Pranav's boss, Appa comes inebriated and embarrasses Pranav's boss. Although the next day Appa apologises, Pranav does not seem to mind it and dismisses it as a one-off incident.

Meanwhile, Appa decides to visit his friend Gangadhar after knowing about the demise of his wife, Lakshmi. He is devastated after the demise of his wife, Lakshmi, which terribly affected his health. The scene that follows at the hospital, is a heart-touching conversation between Karna and Krishna enacted by Gangadhar and Appa respectively while Gangadhar lies on his hospital bed. Mesmerised by Gangadhar's performance and pitying his condition, Appa grants Gangadhar his last wish.

The next day, Appa returns to his son-in-law's house. Vasundhara tells Appa that Gangadhar had overdosed on sleeping pills and that he is no more, to which Appa confesses that he gave the pills to him, implying that it was his last wish.

On one occasion, Appa insults Pranav's boss's son when he cannot stand his weak adaptation of Othello. This irritates Pooja, and she confronts her father. She makes arrangements for them to shift to her outhouse; however, her husband still stands by Appa and regards this as a "not a big deal". Pooja makes sure that the outhouse is well-maintained, and they are taken good care of.

In one instance, Pooja misplaces cash given to her by her husband, and in a turn of events, she accuses her parents of stealing it. This creates a rift between them. Pooja realises her mistake later when she finds the money. She apologises to her parents, but it is too late as Appa and Vasundhara have already decided to move out. Pooja's husband Pranav is still sympathetic to her parents but cannot change their hearts. On that night, they escape from the outhouse to their ancestral village where they have an old house in a dilapidated state. On the way, they halt at a village where Vasundhara dies of fever. Appa is destroyed by this loss. He is supported by a boot polishwala named Raja.

Raja is extremely poor and a homeless person who lives with his family under a bridge. At times, Appa is delusional and suffers from the fact that the grandeur with which he had lived as an actor now makes his pain unbearable, given his state of loneliness and poverty. Appa serves tea at a tea stall where he enthrals his customers with poetry recitals and dialogue from his plays. A man named Siddharth, who has respect and a fondness for the art of acting, continuously follows Appa. For Siddharth, he is a noble actor and an idol. Appa hides his real identity from Siddharth and refuses to acknowledge that he is *'Rangmanch Ka Shahenshah'*. Siddharth's conviction that Appa is a great actor remains unwavered.

One day, Appa reads in the papers that his favourite theatre had burnt down in a fire. He goes there immediately and is completely shattered to see the theatre reduced to ashes. Siddharth also arrives there as he is following Appa. Here Appa starts reliving his old memories and also accepts Siddharth's claim that he is the real Natsamrat Bhalerao. Siddharth reveals that he knew all about him and his past. His family and Raja also come there to find him. They request him to come home with them and to live with them, but he refuses.

Appa is in a delusional state and shuffles between reality and the great personalities he had once portrayed as an actor on the very same stage. He gives his last performance on the theatre stage for Siddharth and says, "Do you understand, dear Siddarth, this is what theatre acting is all about? To fulfil one's longing." He unexpectedly screams by placing a hand on his throat and collapses. Immediately everyone runs to hold him, but they find that he has already departed.

# 4. THE ASPIRATIONS

Amar Apte is a private detective who makes ends meet by spying on cheating partners. He is married to Prachi. She regrets marrying him despite her parents being against this marriage. Amar is not able to make ends meet and is supported by his in-laws.

On one such assignment, he manages to capture a close-up of a woman with her lover, as requested by her husband but gets exposed due to his proximity. Although he escapes the scene, he is visited by cops who tell him that he has messed with the wrong guy. The lover of the lady he had caught earlier is Mr Prasad Sathe, a prominent businessman. He filed a case against Amar for breach of privacy. The police take all his earnings from this case as a bribe to hush up the case.

A few days later, a lady visits Amar who wants to spy on her husband. She introduces herself as Neha, the wife of Prasad Sathe. She hands him the exact amount he had lost bribing the police in advance for the job. When he visits her home to investigate, Neha informs him that Prasad does not stay there and only visits occasionally.

They start meeting regularly on the pretext of discussing Prasad and sharing their deep feelings. Both fall in love with each other. On the other hand, when Amar is spying on Prasad, he finds out the place where he stays and subsequently discovers that Neha is Prasad's mistress while his wife is someone else. Enraged, Amar confronts Prasad with all the evidence and demands the same fee he had lost earlier because of him. Prasad responds that the fee is peanuts for him and he would receive a big paycheck if he did a small job for him.

He meets Neha and tells her not to worry; he assures her husband does not have an affair. One night he argues with Prachi and she admonishes him, saying that no woman would love a man like him who cannot take responsibility for the household. He is enraged and vents out all his frustration on her. He then goes straight to Neha and asks her if a woman would love a man like him. They become entangled in emotions, drawing them closer to each other.

An unknown person calls Prachi and tells her about her husband's affair. She visits Neha's place where she finds them getting close to one another. The next day when Amar returns home, Prachi tells him that she is pregnant and is now ready to forgive him.

Later in the day, Neha meets him at his office which is attached to his home. She asks him about the future of their relationship and tells him that it cannot be a one-night stand. She would reveal the relationship to his wife if he doesn't comply with her. Amar tries to calm her and tells her that they cannot discuss these things at his office. He suggests that they go to her home.

Amar goes through mixed emotions and accepts that he deeply loves her, but at the same time, he cannot be an unfaithful husband or an irresponsible father. Neha gives Amar 15 minutes to take a call, after which she would call Prachi. Amar rushes home to answer that call in the nick of time and then leaves for the funeral of his neighbour who died of old age. Neha visits Amar's home while he is at the funeral. She gives a letter for him to his mother-in-law.

When Amar returns, his mother-in-law tells him that Neha has come to visit him, forgetting about the letter. Amar rushes to Neha's place and tries to explain his position to her. As he is doing that, he turns back to see Neha lying on the floor, profusely bleeding from her head. He does not understand what to do and rushes back home in panic.

The next day, he scans the newspaper for any news, tries calling Neha and visits her place, but there is no trace of Neha. He is surprised by a car honking and when he comes out of her home, he finds a car waiting for him. The driver takes him to a private party hosted by Prasad, which is attended by prominent people (high-ranking police officers, politicians, etc.). They all ask him for his visiting card. He also sees a different girl in the arms of Prasad. At the party, he gives Amar the fat paycheck as promised earlier.

Amar's financial situation improves, and he leads the life of the detective he once dreamt of. His rise makes Prachi and her parents happy. However, Amar suffers from hallucinations, and Neha's voice rings in his ears. One day he happens to find the letter Neha had earlier given to him where she mentioned that with great difficulty she had forgiven him and wanted to move on. If he wishes to lead his life as a responsible husband, then he should never meet her again.

After reading this, he decides to find Neha and meets Prasad to find her whereabouts. He tells him that Neha is already dead and reminds him that it was he who had actually killed her without leaving any trace. Later, he recalls the fat deal he had earlier made with Prasad; it was for getting rid of Neha from his life.

Amar returns home with a heavy heart and finally gathers the courage to tell Prachi that he has committed the murder of Neha and he might be killed anytime. If he doesn't return tomorrow, understand the situation and help him. Prachi is shocked and cannot react to this. However, the next day they both visit the doctor for Prachi's sonography.

# 5. THE DREAMS

Vedant Patel is giving a presentation at a school about the services provided by his sports club. Gopal is released from prison and Vedant picks him up. While halting at a restaurant midway, Vedant and Gopal reminisce about their lives 23 years ago and remember their friend Ansh.

## Twenty-three years ago: Year 2000

Ansh "Ish" Bhatt is an ex-district-level cricketer, a victim of politics in the cricketing selection fraternity. Gopal is the nephew of a Hindu politician, Mannu, who funds his father's temple, and Vedant is a geek with a penchant for business and numbers. Together they open a sports shop and an academy to train and promote talented budding cricketers.

Ansh requests Vedant to teach mathematics to his sister Geeta for her upcoming exams. Vedant is reluctant at first but agrees eventually. Geeta and Vedant gradually come close to each other. Gopal discovers their affair and warns Vedant of the consequences; he is aware that Ansh is very protective of his sister.

The three friends spot Naseem, who has a rare talent for cricket, and Ansh starts training him vigorously. Vedant is ambitious and wants to expand the budding business by opening a shop in a mall in an upcoming area of the city. With financial help coming from Mannu, the trio set up shop in the mall. On 26 January 2001, a destructive earthquake hits

Gujarat, and the mall is destroyed. Vedant is devastated. They are unable to pay back the money they borrowed from Mannu so Gopal is forced to work for Mannu's right-wing party due to the money they owe him. He helps them in providing relief to the people affected by the earthquake.

When the relief camps of Mannu's party decline to give shelter to Muslims in troubled times, Ansh and Gopal quarrel over their politico-religious outlooks and temporarily break off their friendship. They reunite after India's surprise win in the test match against Australia on 15 March 2001.

Thereafter, Gopal gets busy with religious politics and joins Mannu's party while Ansh and Vedant, are busy with Naseem and Geeta respectively. Tension arises in the political sphere when Mannu loses the elections in his constituency to his opponent Amar, who is supported by Naseem's father Imran, a local Muslim leader. As a part of his party's campaign, in 2002, Mannu sent pilgrims to Ayodhya to the Ram Temple. Omi's parents are also among them. On their way back, on 27 February 2002, they learn about the Godhra train massacre. Omi's parents are killed in the incident. The city is engulfed in a full-blown riot where people of both religions are unsafe. Taking advantage of Omi's emotional situation, Mannu convinces him to take revenge on the murderers of his parents.

Ish and Vedant hide in Naseem's house, fearing the communal riots. As expected, the violence starts by sunset, and the mob led by Mannu storms into the Muslim locality, killing every Muslim in sight. A fight ensues between Imran and Mannu, where Imran fatally stabs Mannu in defence and rushes to save Naseem and take shelter in their attic. Omi, enraged at Mannu's death, follows him with a gun. Meanwhile,

Ansh learns of Geeta and Vedant's relationship. Enraged, he goes to Vedant's house to thrash him. While Gopal enters the premises with a gun in hand, desperate to find and kill Naseem and Imran, Ansh and Vedant hurriedly try to stop Omi. But Gopal doesn't budge and shoots Naseem and Imran. Ish, in a bid to save Naseem, takes the bullet himself and consequently dies, leaving both his friends, father, and Geeta devastated.

## Present day: Year 2023

Gopal is released from prison. Vedant and Geeta are married and have a son, whom they have named Ansh after Ish. Geeta forgives Gopal when he breaks down in front of her. Naseem debuts in international cricket and represents India against Australia. He plays his first shot by hitting the ball to the boundary with a cover drive just like Ansh had taught him. Ish's spirit smiles at Naseem's feat and fades away.

# 6. THE BATTLE

Asad Ali, an orphaned extortionist from Dongri, makes a living by intimidating shopkeepers for money. During a confrontation, he gets into a brutal fight and sustains injuries. Seeking medical attention, he arrives at a hospital, where Dr Nirali treats his wounds. However, unimpressed by his violent lifestyle, she sternly criticises him for his actions and orders him to leave. One day, at a local boxing school, Ali comes across a video of Muhammad Ali and decides to start boxing.

He goes to Coach Naravane's aka Nana's boxing school where Nana tests his ability to box. But he is defeated in the match because of his lack of technique. Nana is Nirali's father. When Ali visits the hospital again, Nirali is kinder with him this time as she learns about his humane side. She gets to know that he is involved in taking care of and buying gifts for orphaned children. She couldn't put together these two different personalities of him. She confronts him and asks if he wants to be a boxer or a gangster.

Ali decides to leave behind his life as an extortionist and returns to Nana's boxing school, determined to start anew. With renewed focus, he begins his training in earnest. After months of hard work and intense practice, he earns his boxing licence and starts participating in boxing matches, winning most of them. He is christened "Toofaan" by Nana. He falls in love with Nirali. When Nana finds out about this, he angrily beats Ali, believing that Asad is conning his daughter. But Nirali and Asad are firm in their resolve. Nana disapproves of their relationship, disowns Nirali and throws her out of his house. Asad and Nirali start looking for a home but find it difficult due to their religious differences. The only house that they can stay in requires Asad to return to being a gangster and work for his old boss, which he refuses. Hence, Nirali decides to stay in a women's hostel.

At his next boxing match, Asad is offered a large sum of money to lose, which he does, but is later caught and receives a five-year ban. After reconciling with Nirali, they marry, and sometime later, have a child. They name her Khushi. However, Nana continues to maintain distance from Nirali and does not want anything to do with his grandchild. Asad proves to be an unfit father to Khushi.

After the five-year ban, Asad receives his reinstatement boxing letter but trashes it as he does not want to return to boxing and informs Nirali of his decision. Nirali goes behind his back, completes the formalities, and gets his new boxing licence.

On the way back, Nirali dies in a stampede at a train station. Wanting to fulfil Nirali's dream, Asad returns to boxing and gets back in shape. Meanwhile, Nana begins to spend more time with Khushi after Nirali's death. Asad starts participating in matches and wins most of them.

In a crucial match, the judge, Dharmesh Patil—a former state champion whom Asad had previously defeated—bribes the referee to ensure Asad's loss. Throughout the fight, Asad's opponent lands a series of illegal punches, which the referee deliberately ignores.

Nana visits Patil to discuss this and secretly records him explaining what had happened. Patil is later fired from the boxing federation, and Asad is reinstated as the winner of the match. In the final match, Asad faces Tejas, a fierce fighter known for incapacitating his opponents before the second round even begins. Asad starts losing, struggling against Prithvi's relentless attacks. Just then, Nana returns to his corner and urges him to fight for Nirali. Drawing strength from this, Asad makes a stunning comeback, overpowering Tejas and securing a hard-fought victory.

# 7. THE MARKET

Sameer Khan is a small-time stock trader from New Delhi. He arrives in Mumbai to fulfil his dream of working with his role model, wealthy and ruthless **Gujarati** stock market leader Dhruv Mehta. Dhruv Mehta is known as a "fraud" in business circles.

Sameer bluffs his way into the city's largest trading firm and convinces them to give him a job. He ropes in a high-profile client with the help of his co-worker and girlfriend Meera, thereby beginning a successful career at the firm. When attending an event with Meera, he spots Dhruv Mehta and gives him stock advice that turns out to be profitable, forcing Kothari to hire him. However, Kothari warns him that he cannot afford to lose any of his money. After his first trade with Kothari's funds ends badly, Sameer is desperate not to lose Kothari's account and illegally uses insider information from Meera to recoup Kothari's losses.

Eventually, Sameer grows close to Kothari and his wife, Parul, frequently visiting their mansion and spending leisure time on his yacht with Meera. Meanwhile, Kothari offers Sameer an opportunity to make even more money through the government's latest scheme, which is about to begin accepting bids from telecommunications companies for a new project. Kothari informs Sameer that he has bribed a minister to select an **IT** company called Skycom and the two can make a killing on the deal. Kothari gives Sameer the money to buy Skycom. Sameer convinces his new brother-in-law Farhan to invest all of his savings in Skycom shares, promising him hefty returns. Farhan was sure that the government would select Skycom's bid for their new project. However, Skycom's bid is rejected, and Sameer is ruined. Kothari sells off all of his Skycom shares right before the announcement of the bid winner.

Sameer discovers that Kothari deliberately set him up to take the fall for Skycom for Kothari's monetary profit and that he arranged for Meera to influence him from the beginning. SEBI agents, led by Arvind Mukherjee, detain Sameer for insider trading, though their real target is Kothari. Sameer convinces them that Dhruv has been using old-school methods which will not leave any evidence or trail behind. Using information from Parul, Sameer can prove to the SEBI agents that Kothari has been bribing government ministers with diamonds that are smuggled via **Surat-Mumbai Karnavati Express**. Dhruv is arrested, and his family leaves him. After numerous court hearings, Dhruv is summoned when Meera agrees to testify about the bribes. Sameer questions her, asking why she surrendered herself since he never revealed her name. However, Meera responds by leaving him, saying she deserves this outcome. Dhruv comes out on bail after a month and returns to his empty house, his wife and kids are gone. He calls his secretary and tells him that the market (*Baazaar*) is open, returning to his old ways.

# 8. THE DEAL

Vikram Rajput, a businessman, is involved in an accident due to drunk driving but is saved from death by Arjun Varma. Seeing that Vikram is heavily intoxicated, Arjun hails a taxi and decides to take him home. Once at the Rajput Bungalow, Vikram invites Arjun inside to thank him. He introduces him to his wife, Rhea Kapoor, a glamorous but shady young lady, and his lawyer and friend, Kunal Desai. Grateful for the help, he hires Arjun as his chauffeur, much to the chagrin of Rhea. Desai also develops a dislike for him. Desai and Rhea see Arjun as a threat. Rhea tries her best to get Arjun out of the house by framing him for robbery, but Arjun saves himself with his quick wit and intelligence.

Vikram reveals to Arjun that he is neck-deep in loans and depressed due to his constant drinking, and Rhea wants to kill him to claim his insurance worth 24 crores. One day, Rhea threw his inhaler out of a window when he had an asthma attack. Luckily, Arjun was around and could give it to Vikram in time.

He calls Arjun and Rhea and hands Arjun a letter. He then tells Rhea about a little change he had made in his insurance policy. According to the new conditions of the policy, the insurance money could only be claimed if Vikram is murdered and not if he kills himself. Vikram knew Rhea would try to make his suicide appear to be murder. He also asks Arjun to stay so he cannot be blamed for his death. And he shoots himself!

Rhea rushes to call the police, but Arjun convinces her that together they can prove his suicide to be murder. Arjun offers to collaborate with Rhea on the condition that they will split the insurance money equally. Rhea initially hesitates but ultimately agrees after Arjun reveals a letter he was instructed to deliver to Desai. The letter, written by Vikram, demands that Desai free Rhea from jail if she can prove his death was a murder, and then submit the letter to the insurance company to prevent them from releasing the money to her.

Then they decide to hide Vikram's body in the freezer to stop it from decaying and place Vikram's alcohol bottles on it to divert people's attention from it. They also clear the house of all evidence of Vikram's death. They decide to pretend that Vikram is in his bedroom, too ill to meet anyone and hire a nurse named Savita, whom they can blame for the situation.

When Savita switches the freezer off, Arjun makes an excuse that it must stay on due to its system. Rhea becomes suspicious of Savita after she nearly opens the freezer one night pretending to sleepwalk. Fearing that Savita might uncover their secret, Rhea contemplates killing her. However, Arjun persuades her not to take such drastic action.

Simultaneously, Rhea secretly plans with Desai to kick Arjun out and take the money for themselves. One day, Arjun, pretending to be Vikram, leaves the house with Rhea under the pretext of going to a nursing home. He takes her to a milk booth, ties her up, and leaves the car, making it look as though goons have captured her and kidnapped Vikram. However, Rhea's chair falls in the night and she dies after breaking her spine. She is found by the police in the morning.

ACP Gokhale calls Desai to Vikram's house and questions them about the night of the disappearance. Desai recounts everything he knew and also tells Gokhale that Vikram has not made a will. Gokhale leaves after appointing a police officer behind to remain guard.

Desai then reveals to Arjun that Vikram did make a will and entrusted all of his assets to Arjun to save his life. This makes Arjun the prime suspect. Desai threatens Arjun that he intends to take the will to the police station the next morning. After making the guarding officer drunk, Arjun opens the freezer, but Desai unexpectedly appears and discovers the body. Arjun tells him the truth but claims Rhea planned the whole thing.

Desai decides to take advantage of the situation. He forces Arjun to give him the power of attorney so he can inherit both the insurance money and the will for himself. When Arjun refuses, Desai takes an awoken Savita at gunpoint, but Gokhale and the police arrive. Taking advantage of the situation, Arjun falsely blames Desai for the deaths of Vikram and Rhea. This angers Desai, and he tries to shoot Arjun, but Gokhale shoots and kills him first.

Arjun uses the insurance and will money to build his own luxurious house. Savita reveals that she recognises the shoes "Vikram" was wearing when he left with Rhea for the nursing home. They are the same shoes that Arjun is wearing now. They both laugh, realising they've been caught and decide to become partners.

# 9. THE DESTINATION WEDDINGS

Meera Sharma is a young woman living in Amritsar with her three sisters and parents. The family is invited to a friend's wedding ceremony, where Meera meets Ryan Cooper, a handsome and wealthy American who is a long-time friend of the Indian-British barrister Aryan, and Aryan's sister Tara. Aryan is instantly attracted to Meera's eldest sister Ananya and likewise, Cooper is attracted to Meera. During the wedding reception due to a difference of opinion, Meera takes a dislike to Cooper but when Aryan invites Ananya to Goa, Meera's father asks her to go with them and she eventually agrees to do so. In Goa too, Meera and Cooper are at loggerheads regarding their ideas on men and women and India's economic future. Later that night on the beach, Meera meets Johnny Wickham, Cooper's former friend from London, and he validates her low opinion of Cooper.

A few months later, the Sharma family is visited by Singh Saab, a family friend living in Los Angeles, who has come to India to find a "traditional girl", who he can marry. While Singh Saab is attracted to Ananya, Mrs Sharma steers him towards Meera, making Meera uncomfortable. Wickham is invited to join the family and Singh Saab at the Garba, despite Mrs Sharma's disapproval. Meera happily accepts a dance with Wickham, even as Cooper and Tara warn her against becoming involved with him. Meera angers her mother by turning down a proposal from Singh Saab.

Aryan, Tara, and Cooper are invited to the Sharma house for dinner, where Mrs Sharma furthers her guests' discomfort by commenting loudly on Aryan and Ananya's impending engagement and future babies.

The following day, Aryan visits the house to bid farewell to Ananya and promises to write to her from London. Later, their youngest sister, Riya Sharma, announces that Meera's friend, Priya, is marrying Singh Saab, much to the surprise of both Ananya and, especially, Meera. That same night, Wickham also announces that he is leaving and promises to write to Meera. However, neither Aryan nor Wickham writes to the two older sisters. Instead, Wickham secretly writes to Riya.

Singh Saab and Priya invite the Sharma family to their wedding in Los Angeles, and the family eagerly accepts. Ananya is particularly excited, as she plans to stop over in London, hoping to see Aryan again. In London, Tara informs the Sharma family that Aryan is in New York to meet potential brides, devastating Ananya, Meera, and Mrs Sharma. They were to take a flight to Los Angeles from Heathrow Airport, when Riya, Ananya, Meera and Mrs Sharma coincidentally ran into Cooper, who also happened to be a guest at Singh Saab and Priya's wedding. On board, Cooper offers his first-class seat to Mrs Sharma so he can sit next to Meera in economy class and spend time with her throughout the journey. They stop over in California for a few days. During the time they spent together on the flight and in California, Meera's opinion of Cooper begins to change, and the two fall in love.

At the wedding, Cooper's condescending mother, Catherine, introduces Meera to Cooper's former girlfriend, Emily. Ananya and Meera also meet Cooper's younger sister,

Georgie, who tells Meera that Aryan and Cooper are not in contact because Cooper persuaded Aryan not to marry an Indian girl with a gold-digger mother. Meera realises that Cooper is the reason why Ananya never heard from Aryan and she is furious at him. Unaware of this development, Cooper proposes to Meera, who angrily refuses his proposal and blames him for Ananya's unhappiness.

Back in London, Riya takes advantage of the family's layover to secretly meet Wickham. Meanwhile, Cooper apologises to Meera, telling her that he has helped reconcile Aryan with Ananya. Meera realises that Cooper was right about Wickham and asks for his help to find Riya. Cooper reveals that Wickham had many other girlfriends besides Georgie and that he had tried to marry Georgie for her family's money. When his plan fell through, he ran away. Together, Cooper and Meera rescue Riya, and she finally accepts Cooper's proposal. Finally, Ananya marries Aryan, and Meera marries Cooper.

# 10. THE AUSPICIOUS MOMENT

An NRI producer and former leading actress, **Aparna Dutta**, has returned to India to invest in a film. She organises an event to announce her new venture. Her second husband **Anirban Basu**, an out-of-work director, is assigned to direct this new film. **Aparna** insists on casting the retired actress, **Madhavi Sen**, in a prominent role. Covering the event are a journalist for a local magazine, **Tuhina Choudhury**, and a freelance photographer, **Indranil Choudhury**. The production team also includes makeup artist **Nandini Ghosh** and camera assistant Sunil Mehra.

At the reception, **Madhavi** feels unwell and leaves early. She takes **Tuhina** home with her and agrees to interview her. At her house, however, **Madhavi**'s condition deteriorates until she collapses and dies. Learning from her husband that she was a drug addict, police suspect an overdose, but the autopsy reveals strychnine poisoning. The investigating officer Arindam Chatterjee initially suspects the husband, who is in an extramarital affair, but the poison is found to have entered her system while she was at the reception event. **Tuhina** reveals that **Madhavi** only had a glass of soft drink at the party, and the drink was actually meant for **Aparna**, meaning that she was the real target. **Tuhina** discusses all this with her paternal aunt, Ranga Pishima, who conjectures that another murder might soon follow.

Meanwhile, a mutual attraction develops between **Tuhina** and Arindam and **Tuhina** and **Indranil**. **Pishima** discovers that **Indranil** is actually related to **Aparna**: his uncle was **Aparna**'s first husband, and she doted on **Indranil** when he was a child.

**Nandini** tells **Aparna** about her relationship with Sunil, who is married, and how Sunil is refusing to pay for the treatment of **Nandini**'s daughter. **Aparna** promises to help her and tells her about her own son, who died aged 16 from a congenital disorder. **Nandini** goes to Sunil's house, where she is seen leaving after having a soft drink. Later, she is found dead, and Sunil is arrested in connection with her death.

**Pishima** listens to the recordings of **Tuhina**'s interview with **Madhavi**, questions **Indranil** further about **Aparna**, and then asks **Tuhina** to call up the director of **Madhavi** and **Aparna**'s last film together. She then writes an anonymous piece in her niece's magazine on whether infections during pregnancy can harm the unborn child, in the edition which is to carry **Aparna**'s interview with **Tuhina**. A copy is sent to **Aparna** with the page highlighted. This has the desired effect as **Aparna** rushes to **Pishima** and **Tuhina**'s home to enquire about the piece, and **Pishima** narrates to her how she solved the mystery.

During their last film together, **Aparna** was pregnant and **Madhavi** had a contagious disease, which she spread to her co-actress. This infection was transmitted to the unborn child, who unfortunately did not survive. **Aparna** poisoned **Madhavi** in revenge but was seen by **Nandini**, who tried to blackmail her and was silenced in turn.

**Pishima** tells **Aparna** that she is her fan and that her story is safe with her. **Aparna** returns home and is later found to have committed suicide. As per her last promise, she sends **Pishima** an autograph and a long reply to her fan mail, in which she also promises to support the treatment of **Nandini**'s daughter.

Torn between Arindam and him, **Tuhina** asks **Indranil** if it is possible to love two people at once. **Indranil** responds by recalling that **Aparna** once asked him the same question before leaving his uncle for **Anirban**. He explains that **Aparna** proved it was impossible, as she completely forgot about him after her son was born, to the extent that she didn't even recognise him at the reception.

# 11. THE MEETING BY CHANCE

Ravi is a poor countryman, who lives in Bhagalpur. He recently lost his job and ventures to start a business of his own. He goes to the city to see if he can arrange some money. In the city, he stays with his friends, Alok and Sheela, who help him in his desperate quest to arrange money. Alok makes some phone calls and writes a letter for him that he can send to his former classmates. The letter explains Ravi's plight and asks for any money to spare. Ravi, ashamed, tells Alok to forget the letter and that he will go out the next day and ask for money personally.

The next morning, over breakfast, Alok talks about his career as a producer for TV serials. Ravi asks Alok for the address of a place he plans to visit while looking for money that day. It turns out to be the address of a woman Ravi was once supposed to marry, but he ended up marrying someone else instead. Alok remembers what he had to go through to get Ravi over her and insists he not go there and upset himself. Sheela tells Alok not to get so angry and allows Ravi to do what he pleases. The woman is supposed to be quite wealthy, and Ravi hopes not only to see her again (for the first time since her marriage) but perhaps to get some money as well. Alok finally backs off.

As Ravi prepares to leave, Alok gives him an address book of the people from whom he may be able to borrow money, while Sheela gives Ravi a mobile phone and teaches him to use it, and a raincoat to keep him dry. On his journey,

Ravi manages to collect 12,000 rupees before stopping and reaching the home of his lost love, Sunita. As Ravi reaches her house, he is reminded of a time when they were together and happy. However, he is interrupted by Sunita's voice. At first, she doesn't believe it's really him and takes some time before finally opening the door. When she does, she tells him that she fell asleep and warmly invites him. There is no one home. Sunita's husband is away, and the servants are out playing cards.

While sitting, she tells him that he has changed—his hair is missing, he's gotten darker and lost weight. He asks her to switch on a light so he can see her better because she does not look well. She goes inside but forbids him to follow her into the house. She brings the light and shows her face, free of bruises or black eyes, and assures him that her husband really loves her. He asks her why she wears such an expensive sari around the house, and she says it would just sit there otherwise since she never leaves the house.

Sunita is very paranoid and never opens the door for fear of burglars in her dangerous town coming to invade her wealthy home. She says her husband is away to Japan on business and offered for her to come but she refused because of a fear of being locked in a bathroom and not knowing English. Ravi laughs and tells her she hasn't changed a bit.

The doorbell soon rings, and Ravi insists on answering it. Sunita gets very afraid and urges him to let it be because she doesn't want to be seen home alone with another man while her husband is away and for word to get to him. He starts to answer the door anyway, and she gets very upset, so he sits down. Ravi has a flashback to the time he fell ill upon hearing about Sunita's marriage. He was still deeply in love with her at that moment.

Later, Sunita asks what Ravi does for a living, and he says that he produces serials. In fact, he is the owner of the company. He tells her that he and his mother live in a two-storey apartment and that she should visit them sometime. Of course, this is far from true; he suddenly has a flashback of him bringing his mother a portable toilet just so she won't have to walk far to use it. Sunita asks if he is married, and he hints that his mother has a girl set up. Sunita doesn't seem pleased.

Another flashback reveals that, although very sick from a fever, Ravi had an outburst during Sunita's engagement when he demanded it be broken off. He tells her that he can support her; he'll find a way.

Back in the present, Sheela calls him on his mobile to see how he is and if he has eaten. When Sunita asks who it was, he says that it was his secretary. Sunita asks, "Is she beautiful and intelligent?" To which Ravi replies, "She's pretty and fluent in English." She accuses him of flirting. When she asks if he has eaten, she quickly realises that she has neglected to feed him. He reassures her that it's not necessary, but she insists on going out to get him food, as she doesn't think he'll like what's available in the house. She tells him not to answer the door for anyone, takes his raincoat, and leaves.

While she is gone, he has a flashback of her engagement, and him begging her one last time not to marry, and to stay with him. It is interrupted by a man at the window, begging to be let in to use the bathroom. Ravi reluctantly lets him in, but after he uses it he refuses to leave. Suspicious, Ravi confronts him and he reveals that he is the landlord. The landlord mistakes Ravi for being the tenant. Ravi wondered why a couple so rich would need to rent. The landlord then reveals that Sunita and her husband are not rich at all. In fact, they are close to being evicted from their home for lack of paying rent. The landlord even shows Ravi the bathroom, which he was refused access to, and sees how empty and dirty it is, like the bathroom of a very poor family. He is confused, for he remembers when Sunita got married, the wedding was very expensive and her husband had a very nice job. The landlord reveals that Sunita's husband lost all his wealth in a scam and has been a conman ever since, scamming others for money. Ravi understood the reason he was not home and why Sunita never opened the door. She feared bill collectors and those who wanted to throw them out of their homes. Very alarmed, Ravi gives the landlord the 12,000 rupees he collected to pay three months' rent and makes the man promise not to throw her out immediately.

Ravi writes her a letter telling her that he now knows the truth and what he has done to help her. He also says that had they been married, he would have done so anyway. He puts the letter under a sofa cover. Sunita returns and says that the shopkeeper was sleeping and she had to wake him up, which is why she took so long. He eats the food she brought and continues to lie about his profession and lifestyle. She says, "I feel trapped in the house. I want to go far away, even if it means getting stuck in the aeroplane bathroom."

Ravi says that even if that were to happen, someone like him would be there to let her out. She doesn't want to be given false hope and starts to cry. He tries to comfort her by shifting the conversation to his business. She also tells him that they are going to be moving into a bigger house and that he should visit when he returns. After finishing his meal, he

asks to wash his hands. Once again, Sunita refuses to let him
see the rest of the house and goes to get him a finger bowl.
He rinses his hands and then wipes them on the sofa cover,
prompting Sunita to scold him. He apologises and tells her to
have it washed.

# 12. THE OCCASION

Ramesh Chadda and his wife Sunita have arranged a marriage for their daughter Meera to Arjun Mehta. Arjun is the son of a family friend who lives in Texas, and Meera has only known him for a few weeks. As so often happens in Indian culture, such a wedding means that the extended family comes together from all corners of the globe, bringing its emotional baggage along.

Sunita's sister Shashi and her husband CL, who arrived earlier from Australia, help Ramesh and Sunita in organising the wedding. A few days before the engagement, Mahesh Kapoor, Ramesh's extremely wealthy brother-in-law, arrives from the US. Mahesh is married to Ramesh's sister and has helped the Chadda family regain their financial footing after the partition of India left them penniless decades ago. Mahesh offers to pay for Meera's cousin, Neha Chadda's education at a university in the US after the family consults him for advice. Neha and her mother live with the Chadda family, who took them in after the death of Neha's father. Despite his generous offer, Neha stays away from Mahesh and is not comfortable in his presence.

As the planning for the wedding progresses, Ramesh begins experiencing difficulty in paying for the final, smaller aspects of the wedding and is embarrassed when he has to borrow money from friends and colleagues.

Meanwhile, PK Dubey, the eccentric wedding planner, falls in love with Emma, the Chaddas' maid. One day, Dubey's workers see Emma trying on Meera's wedding jewellery, and the men accuse her of stealing. The incident causes her to become withdrawn from Dubey, and he grows depressed. Eventually, the workers apologise to Emma, and she reconciles with Dubey.

Meanwhile, Rohan, Meera's younger brother, enthusiastically prepares an elaborate dance performance for the pre-wedding celebrations alongside his cousin, Simran Sharma. However, their father, Ramesh, worries that Rohan's interests make him appear too effeminate and secretly considers sending him to boarding school. The night before the ceremony, Rohan refuses to dance due to the comments made by his father, and Simran performs with the help of Rahul, Sunita's nephew from Australia.

A few days before the wedding, Meera sleeps with an old lover, her married boss Rajiv, and confesses this to Arjun. The incident only serves as a reminder to Meera as to why she stopped seeing Rajiv. Though he is initially angry, Arjun is glad for her honesty and is confident that they can put it behind them and be happy together. Meera and Arjun grow closer, and they share a few intimate moments, which reaffirm their faith in the marriage.

Neha is alarmed when she observes what seems to be Mahesh grooming a younger relative, ten-year-old Aliya, and grows increasingly concerned about his behaviour. After a night of jokes, drama, and dances, Neha catches Mahesh trying to take Aliya for a drive alone. Neha stops them from driving off and takes Aliya away from her, revealing to Ramesh and others that Mahesh had molested her as a child. Ramesh's sister does not believe her, attributing her accusations to her character and unmarried status. Emotionally distraught, Neha leaves.

The next day, Ramesh pleads with Neha to return to the wedding, admitting that he can't possibly imagine what she has gone through, at the same time he also explains that he can't disown Mahesh since they are family. Neha is not happy but agrees to return for the sake of Meera. Hours before the wedding, however, Ramesh changes his mind and tells his sister and Mahesh to leave the wedding and the family home. Mahesh's wife insists that Neha's accusation is a small matter, but Ramesh stands his ground.

The monsoon rains begin as Meera and Arjun are married in an elaborate wedding, while Dubey and Emma simultaneously wed in a simple ceremony, and later celebrate with the Chaddas. Neha moves on from her past life and is finally able to enjoy the festivities freely.

# 13. THE CONCERNS

A tender romance blossoming in Kolkata between law student Suraj and his friend's sister Jaya is nipped suddenly when his father sends an urgent and mysterious summons from his village home. There, the dutiful son is peremptorily ordered to marry Sharda, the daughter of a helpless widow. Suraj refuses to marry her and confesses that his heart belongs to another. But the widow's fervent plea softens him, and he concedes, albeit with a heavy heart. The wedding takes place, and Suraj sets out with his bride on a riverboat journey back to Kolkata.

Soon a fierce storm arises; the boat tosses helplessly and finally capsizes in the churning waters. Later that night, Suraj comes to his senses on a deserted shore under a starlit sky. Some distance away, he sees the unconscious form of a young bride. Her pulse is still beating, and she responds to him when he calls her 'Sharda'. There is no one else in sight, alive or dead. The two move off and take a train to Kolkata. The bride is wondering why they are not going to Kashi, but she trusts his judgement implicitly.

Jaya, his true love, knows nothing of all this. Suraj has been missing since the evening of her birthday party. She knew about his hasty departure from the city, but nothing else. Though she pines inwardly, she is confident that he will return soon.

Back in Suraj's new home in Kolkata, the facts of mistaken identity gradually come to light. She gets to know that she is Suma, not Sharda. Her husband is a doctor named Shiv Chatterjee. Suraj writes an advertisement to trace his whereabouts, but he does not have the heart to break this news of not finding her husband to the helpless, trusting young girl in his care. He puts her into a boarding school instead. But soon, Jaya's would-be suitor Neel discovers Suraj's secret and brings proof positive to Jaya. Suraj, unable to handle such a scandal, seeks to hide in Gorakhpur with Suma. A devastated Jaya is brought to Kashi by her father to help her forget Suraj. There she meets Shiv, and they warm up to each other.

In the meanwhile, having read the advertisement in an old newspaper, Suma realises the enormity of the lie she has been living and walks out, determined to drown herself in the river. Suraj returns and finds her suicide note and searches everywhere to no avail. He does not know that she has been rescued by a courtesan and deposited in Kashi under Shiv's mother's care. Suma now sees her real husband for the first time but cannot speak up, for he is betrothed to Jaya.

Finally, the advertisement she keeps knotted in her sari is discovered, and the whole truth comes to light. Suraj finally traces Shiv and arrives at his house, where he finds Jaya getting engaged to Shiv.

# 14. THE SEARCH

At Interpol's office in Lyon, a prominent city in France, an officer is looking at reports about Khureshi-Ab'ram, a mysterious international criminal involved in transcontinental trade. He receives a message from the CIA, stating that they suspect a diamond-gold nexus is operating in collaboration with African warlords. Attached to the message is a rear-view image of a person taken in Istanbul on April 7, 2006. The officer dials Interpol's secure phone line and says: Flag it off. It's Ab'ram. Khureshi – Ab'ram.

Meanwhile, in Kerala, CM RD Menon alias "RDM", the leader of the ruling party, Indian Union Front (IUF), dies in the hospital while getting treated at the Mediyal Institute of Medical Science and Research, which turns out to be the opposition leader Mediyal Rajan's daughter's hospital. Taking advantage of the situation and believing that it would benefit the upcoming election, acting CM Arvind Varma sent party workers to riot outside the hospital. Shankar, a truth-seeker, records a Facebook livestream and condemns those who praise RDM, claiming that he was a puppet during his final years in the hands of a financial syndicate, which controls the entire Indian political system. He claims that the IUF party has twice the amount of money than the entire state's treasury, and the person who replaces RDM is crucial. He lists four possible candidates during the livestream: Anjali Ramdas Nair, Rohan Ramdas, Dev Nair, Arvind, and Stephen Nedumpally.

Anjali and Rohan are RDM's children. Anjali has a college-going daughter, Simi, from her first husband, Raghu, who died in a car accident in Dubai seven years ago. She married Dev, a notorious and discreet drug dealer, who mainly deals with real estate and Hawala scams. He is also in contact with drug lords in Mumbai. All his activities are unknown to Anjali. Rohan lives in the US and not much is known about him. Arvind declares himself as the most likely successor to RDM due to his seniority in the party and particularly his lobbying skills. Stephen Nedumpally is a mysterious person promoted by RDM. Stephen was not known until the last six years. Shankar describes him as the "most dangerous person from the list capable of both saving and destroying Kerala and addresses him as Lucifer. Stephen's past is unknown but is known for his post-war reconstruction in Iraq and Afghanistan as well as gold smuggling from Dubai to Kerala—the information that Shankar gathered from dark web research.

Shankar questions why RDM endorsed such a person, accompanying him to every venue and even vacating his consecutively won assembly seat of Nedumpally for him last year. Meanwhile, in Mumbai, Dev meets his partner, Abdul, and tells him that RDM had given him an ultimatum to stop drug trafficking a month ago. With RDM's demise, Dev plans to fund the IUF party with drug money, overthrowing present financier Manappattil Chandy by offering him money three times as initially promised. With the help of Abdul, Dev cuts a deal with drug boss Salim, who agrees to transfer ☐ 250 crore (US$30 million) every month in exchange for importing unchecked drug contraband into Kerala, once the IUF wins the election. Dev must first establish a drug production plant, and Abdul insists that it be set up in the government-sealed timber factory in the Nedumpally range. Meanwhile, in Kerala, the last rites of RDM take place, for which Anjali requests Arvind to prevent Stephen from attending the ceremony.

On Arvind's orders, city commissioner Mayilvahanam attempts to hinder his way but fails. Rohan, who should be performing RDM rituals, is absent—last informed to be on a camping trip. On that night, Dev convenes a meeting with the IUF ministers, informing his decision to fund the party and dissolve the current ministry, which will ensure the preponement of the elections so that they can take advantage of the present sympathy wave and nominate Rohan as the party's next CM candidate. Since Chandy is Stephen's ally, Arvind advises Dev to negotiate with Stephen, but Stephen objects to funding the party with drug money and threatens Dev. Enraged, Dev assigns Vikram, who is the chief of the IUF-funded news network NPTV, to start a smear campaign against Stephen, much to the chagrin of his co-worker and wife Arundathi. A reporter is sent to Shankar to collect evidence based on his claims.

Shankar doesn't have the evidence but claims Chandy is backed by the Khureshi-Ab'ram gang, a nexus that controls the gold-diamond trade around the world and hands over a file named Shankar's X-Files containing pieces of evidence against Dev. Vikram delivers the evidence to Dev, while Shankar is captured by IUF activist Murugan and is confined to an asylum. Dev sends men to the timber factory. Upon knowing this, Stephen kills six of them and defeats the rest. Stephen's aide and Dev's mole Binoy espies the incident and reports it to Arvind and Dev. Mayilvahanam is sent to detect evidence from the premises but finds nothing. From Anjali's diary, Dev finds out that she resents Stephen because her father brought him home and gave more care to him. He was the cause of a rift between her parents. Stephen runs Ashrayam, a destitute home. Binoy persuades one of the inmates, Aparna, to slander Stephen.

On NPTV, she accuses Stephen of smuggling contraband and other illegal activities. This creates public outrage against Stephen, who is arrested and imprisoned. In prison, Stephen gets a phone call from his mercenary and confidant Zayed Masood. Rohan arrives and impresses the public with his speech. While transferring funds to Dev, Salim's containers are sabotaged by Zayed and his cohorts, who demand the release of Stephen. Dev agrees, but Arvind meets Lokesh to arrange a hit on Stephen by his party goons in prison; the attempt fails. Left with no choice, Arvind releases him. Meanwhile, Simi is hospitalised after an LSD overdose. Mayilvahanam blackmails Anjali for a relationship in exchange for not filing a case against Simi.

From Simi, Anjali learns of Dev's predatory behaviour towards her. When asked, Dev admits and threatens to expose Simi's contacts with drug peddlers and threatens to kill her and Simi like Raghu and RDM. Aparna admits on NPTV that she lied about Stephen. With no other choice, Anjali seeks the help of Stephen, who vows to protect them. Stephen's men kill Mayilvahanam and meet Vikram to clear NPTV's debts, giving control of the channel to Anjali. She and Rohan convene a press conference to expose Dev's illegal trades. Rohan tells Dev that his and Anjali's allegiances are with Stephen. Dev is captured in Mumbai by Salim's men. Before Salim can kill him, Zayed and his gang kill them, rescuing Dev for Stephen to kill. Revealing himself to be Stephen's spy, Murugan kills Binoy.

Shankar is released and reunited with his wife and daughter, and Rohan is elected as the new CM.

Stephen meets Zayed and his gang in a remote location in Russia and attends a phone call from a gold-diamond trafficker, Sanghani, to whom he reveals himself as Khureshi-Ab'ram.

# 15. THE DETERMINATION

Anjali and Raghav are a married couple and corporate businesspeople in Gurugram. One night, they are enjoying a party when Anjali receives a telephone call from her office. She leaves for her office but is attacked by thugs who smash her car's window. Anjali escapes but is shaken by the incident. Raghav buys Anjali a gun for self-protection.

One day, Raghav suggests a road trip for Anjali's upcoming birthday. The couple starts their journey the next day while stopping at a roadside dhaba for lunch, where a young woman called Aarti arrives and pleads for help; Aarti tells the couple that she and her husband are about to be murdered. Anjali and Raghav see a gang of men round up Aarti and a young man, beat them, and drag them into their vehicle. Raghav intervenes but Kamal, the gang leader, slaps him and tells him Aarti is his own sister.

Raghav drives after the gang; he and Anjali witness the ongoing honour killing: Aarti and the young man are beaten up, and Aarti is poisoned by Kamal. Raghav and Anjali escape, but the gang soon finds them. As the gang digs a grave for their victims, Kamal uses Anjali and Raghav's gun to shoot Aarti and the man in front of them. A fight ensues, and Raghav shoots a gang member and runs away with Anjali.

At night, one of the gang members finds Raghav and Anjali and injures Raghav. Anjali shoots the gangster dead. Anjali leaves Raghav to get help. She finds a police station and asks the officer for help, but he rejects her when she says she has witnessed an honour killing. Outside, she meets an inspector in his SUV and they drive back to find Raghav. Anjali then realises that the inspector is connected with the attackers; she kills the inspector and drives off in his car. However, she is chased by the gang.

Anjali finds a hut and goes inside to hide. The hut's occupants hide Anjali from a gang member who comes asking about her; they advise Anjali to seek help from the sarpanch (chief) of the nearby village. Anjali tells the village's chief, Ammaji, her entire story. As she completes her story, Anjali sees a pillow cover with the word Aarti stitched on it on Ammaji's lap and a picture of Aarti in the room.

Soon after this, Ammaji locks Anjali in the room, calls the gang, and hands Anjali over to them. Kamal drags her out in front of Ammaji and beats her ruthlessly by slapping her repeatedly and also punches her hard in the stomach. However, Anjali manages to escape with the gang's SUV by threatening to harm Kamal's son and rushes to the railway bridge where she finds that Raghav has been murdered. Grief-stricken, Anjali returns to the village to avenge Raghav's death; she drives the SUV at the gang members and kills them. Ammaji arrives and finds the dead men; she justifies to Anjali that Aarti was her daughter who broke the rules and needs to be punished. Anjali defends herself by telling Ammaji that Raghav was her husband and they killed him and needed to be punished.

# 16. THE ARROGANCE

Rohan Nair is a popular actor in the Malayalam film industry. He always has his manager Mathew Cherian and his makeup man-cum-driver Pillai by his side. All of his previous films have been superhits and as a result, he lives off a superstar status in the industry. Rohan is notorious as a very irresponsible and arrogant person, always partying, and not showing up to shoot locations on time. Due to the same reasons, his last three films have flopped, and the crew of his next film, which is directed by Rahul Dev, aren't confident about the output of the film. Rahul tries calling Rohan, but he doesn't pick up the call as he is busy partying.

One day, Rohan comes home and finds a script for a film in which he is supposed to star and is directed by George, an acclaimed director who is very strict on set. Rohan goes to the set the next day and acts with his co-actor Sanjay. George lashes out at Rohan due to his inability to portray emotions convincingly on-screen during the shot and abuses him. An angry Rohan storms out of the set and while driving away in his car, injures one of the crew members of the film. This causes significant damage to Rohan's self-image, so Rohan, Pillai, and Mathew decide to leave for Dubai and stay there until the issue cools down while George has to shelve his film.

After returning from Dubai, Mathew suggests that Rohan meet Guru, an acting coach, to help out with weak areas in acting and improve them so that his films can fare better.

They meet Guru, who agrees to help Rohan. The next day, Guru meets Rohan in his caravan and tries to tell him how to perform his role, but Rohan, who is intoxicated, tells Guru that he can do it on his own and sends him out. During the shot, Rohan is unable to act properly, but when Guru goes to help him, Rohan tells him to go away as he doesn't want anyone to know that he has hired an acting coach. He feels it will damage his public image. He introduces Guru as his driver who had driven the car the day a crew member from director George's set was injured. Later, after the shot is over, Rohan cancels his contract with Guru in frustration and sends him back. Rohan then calls his ex-girlfriend and former co-star Ann Bava and tells her that his career is declining. Ann tells him to stop going behind girls and avoid drinking, which has become his favourite pastime and also tells him to focus on his acting career instead. She also tells him to stop seeing himself as a superstar but as an actor instead and listen to what the other crew members tell him to do.

After his call with Ann, Rohan realises his mistake and decides to get Guru back. Guru agrees to help him once again. Then, Guru helps Rohan on the set of his films and his acting significantly improves. Once, during a press conference, Rohan tells his fans that his films have been flopping lately and asks them which one of his performances they think is his best to date. He realises that they don't have an answer as none of his performances have been impactful in reality. Guru also tells Rohan to forget about his superstar status and start treating himself as an actor.

As the days go by, Rohan gets a chance to act in a film directed by his mentor, Govind Menon. Rohan goes to act in the film, but as the shoot progresses, a few locals come to the set and start creating a commotion. In the process, they attack the director and some other crew members. The shoot gets called off because of this. Later, as they are sitting in their room, a frustrated and drunk Rohan yells at Guru and Pillai and verbally abuses both of them. Guru is heartbroken and cuts off all ties with Rohan and leaves. Pillai also feels dejected and leaves. Meanwhile, Rohan starts to feel guilty about shouting at Guru and doesn't eat anything for a few days. His guilt of mistreating Guru and Pillai and the pain of losing his mother help him deliver one of his best performances in an emotional sequence for his new film. He tells Mathew that he's done making bad films and that he wants a hit film somehow.

Rohan then decides to mend things with both George and Guru. He goes to George's house and apologises for his behaviour on George's set earlier. That night, he decides to patch things up with Ann and goes to her house with a cake. But as he opens the cake to cut it with her, he gets a call from one of his fans who informs him that he is about to commit suicide due to love failure. Rohan rushes to save his life. He reaches there and sees that the person hasn't jumped yet, but due to the excitement of seeing Rohan, the person accidentally slips from the bridge and falls underwater. Rohan also jumps underwater to save the person's life, but that person ends up saving Rohan's life instead due to the latter's inability to swim underwater. Rohan then takes the person to his house and gives him a place to stay.

The next night, Rohan goes to Guru's house to apologise to him. Guru tells him that he never had any grudge against Rohan and treats him with a biriyani. Rohan then tells Guru that he wants the latter to come back with him, to which Guru replies that there is no point in him coming back as his job as Rohan doesn't need anyone's help now. A few days later, Rohan resumes shooting on director George's film and nails the first shot itself.

# 17. THE REVENGE

ACP Daniel Mathew finds his life shattered when a fake police call lures him away, leading to the brutal death of his wife Rebecca and daughter Sarah. The main culprit is Karan, who wants to avenge Mathew for arresting him in a narcotics case. Karan confesses to killing Rebecca and Sarah, cutting them into pieces and burying their body parts somewhere in a forest but claims he doesn't remember exactly where because he was on a high due to drugs. Mathew gets distraught about his family's death and struggles to find closure because their bodies are never found.

Three years later, Mathew, who is haunted by hallucinations and insomnia, investigates a series of murders with his subordinates SI Neha Nair and Joseph. The two killers, one driving a pickup truck and the other posing as a surgeon, leave cryptic notes at the crime scenes. They name the killer as "Birthday killer." As the team unravels the connections, they discover Hari, a man using an artificial larynx, as a key suspect. They also learn that Hari was a child prodigy singer who lost his voice in surgery.

Delving into the past, Mathew discovers a shared history among the victim's parents: Rajeev and Gopi were postgraduate medical students at Kozhikode Medical College in 1989. Rajeev, Gopi, a retired police surgeon Joseph Kurian, and Samuel were all found to have been friends and PG batchmates. Apparently, they had gotten into an accident, after which they parted ways. Hari is captured while he kidnaps

Samuel. But even as Hari is in Mathew's custody, Joseph is kidnapped. As the truth surfaces, the real Samuel is revealed to be another person. Samuel is arrested as soon as he inflicts the first cut on Joseph's body to kill him. Once in custody, Samuel narrates the flashback to Mathew and his team.

Samuel was a dedicated PG student at the surgery department of Kozhikode Medical College. Joseph was another PG student of surgery, but not as good a surgeon as Samuel; he is jealous of Samuel. Rajeev, a PG student of General Medicine, despises Samuel for being in a relationship with a first-year MBBS student Suja Jayadev whom Rajeev had been pursuing. Gopi, a PG student of anaesthesia, and a junkie who used to be on drugs even while on duty, was found using drugs from the operation theatre stock by Samuel. Samuel reports this to the college authorities, and Gopi is dismissed. Professional jealousy of Joseph, fuelled by Rajeev, leads to Joseph orchestrating a failed surgery resulting in Hari losing his voice forever. Samuel reports Joseph's intentional act to seniors, and Joseph, as well as Samuel being the first assistant at the surgery, are suspended from college. Joseph is blacklisted by his professors and banned from operating a living human being again.

Gopi, Joseph, and Rajeev then go ahead to severely injure Samuel, leading him into a coma. They made up an accident scene, faked injuries on themselves, and told everyone that a drunk Samuel took them for a drive and crashed the car. Samuel lies in a vegetative state for months, and Suja goes into deep depression seeing this. One day, doctors suggest that they remove Samuel's life support and allow him to die peacefully. Suja is heartbroken and in a fit of emotion, she commits suicide by jumping in front of a moving bus. In a fateful irony, Samuel survives life support removal and with years and years of nursing care, regains movement, although he had dissociative amnesia, causing him to forget most of the events of his PG time, including Suja and the cruelty done by Joseph and his friends.

One day, Samuel sees a TV programme featuring Hari, wherein some old videos of him singing are shown. This triggers his memories, and Samuel slowly recollects all the past events. He learns about Suja's death and meets up with Hari who had become wayward after losing his voice, and together they plan the murders. The motive behind the murders was to seek revenge on those who ruined their lives.

Back to the present, Joseph meets Samuel and Hari in Mathew's custody and has no remorse at all. Mathew feels very bad about saving Joseph and says that he needs to die. A surprising turn occurs as Joseph dies on stage at the release ceremony of his autobiography. The forensic surgeon Ramesh Pillai reveals to Mathew that Samuel had poisoned Joseph and the victims with methylene blue and agar-agar, a bacteria-infected surgical ink before making cuts on his body. Later, Rajeev is found dead in his car, while Gopi becomes an alcoholic. His wife leaves him realising that he caused their son's murder.

On his routine visit to Karan in prison, Mathew encounters Samuel and Hari in the prison. Samuel cryptically utters "Bone Residue," hinting at an unresolved truth about Mathew's family. Mathew confronts Karan, realising that there is no bone residue on the weapon he allegedly used in the murders. Karan challenges Mathew to dig deeper for the truth.

# 18. THE BETRAYALS

Karan Malhotra is a toilet paper sales executive in Mumbai, who is leading an unexciting life professionally and personally. One day, to surprise his wife, Nisha Malhotra, he arrives early from the office. He finds his wife getting intimate with another man named Vikram Khanna. Without doing anything, Karan leaves and decides to follow Vikram to find out more about him.

Vikram is married to Simran Mehta, whose father is wealthy. Karan blackmails Vikram after gathering personal information about him. To pay Karan, Vikram gets the money from Simran. When Simran's father demands repayment, Vikram, in turn, blackmails Nisha. Meanwhile, Karan confides in his colleague Arun about his scheme. Nisha approaches Karan for money, claiming it is for her father's treatment. Karan gives her the money after extorting more from Vikram. Nisha then hides the money in a dustbin, which Karan later retrieves.

Arun, who has a crush on Swati, a colleague, takes her on a date and reveals Karan's plans. The very next day, Swati blackmails Karan for money. Karan confronts Arun and then asks Vikram for money. Vikram, in turn, asks Nisha for money, and Nisha asks Karan for the money. From the cash received earlier, Karan sends the amount to Nisha's account, while Nisha puts the money in a dustbin. Vikram collects it and throws it in a dustbin, which Karan collects and gives to Swati.

On Nisha's advice, Vikram hires a detective, Chawla, to catch the blackmailer. Swati blackmails Karan again for more money, but he visits her apartment to confront her, and they argue. Swati slips on her own during the argument and dies. Incidentally, Swati's parents arrive at the apartment at the same time. Karan manages to escape by wearing a mask made out of a paper bag.

The next morning, the police arrive and interrogate everyone in the office. Arun threatens Karan that he will reveal everything to the police because he believes that Karan has killed Swati. Upon interrogation, Karan reveals to the police that Arun liked Swati. Karan convinces Arun to hide the truth from the police. Using Arun's car, Karan purchases the same bag he used the night Swati died and hides it in Arun's car. This makes the police arrest Arun. Arun panics and reveals everything about Karan to the police, but they don't believe him entirely. Meanwhile, Chawla calls Karan telling him he knows about his ruse.

The police then interrogate Karan. Simran follows Vikram and sees him watching a movie with Nisha. Arun is released from police custody and confronts Karan in a heated fight. However, Karan pacifies him by appealing to his greed for money. Karan meets Chawla, who begins blackmailing him for money. Meanwhile, when Vikram returns home, Simran attempts to kill him. In the struggle, Vikram shoots her dead. Shocked, he hides her body. Karan then blackmails Vikram for money to pay off Chawla, threatening to expose him for murdering Simran. Desperate, Vikram turns to Nisha for more money, and Nisha, in turn, asks Karan. However, this time, Karan refuses.

Karan becomes suspicious of Nisha's claims about her father's treatment and decides to follow her. He watches her sell her jewellery and then places the cash in a dustbin at a mall. As he attempts to retrieve it, Vikram arrives first and takes the money. Karan, capturing the moment, takes pictures of Vikram with the cash. Vikram, determined to catch the blackmailer, hides the money in the dustbin and waits. Meanwhile, Karan bribes a security guard to remove the money, but Vikram fails to stop him. Karan retrieves the cash and hands it over to Chawla. Karan then instructs Chawla to call Vikram and falsely claim that the blackmailer is Arun. Enraged, Vikram kills Arun. Karan sends the pictures of Vikram taking the money to Nisha. Meanwhile, Simran's parents report Vikram to the police when they discover he murdered their daughter.

Back at home, heartbroken Nisha deletes Vikram's contact from her phone and messages Karan asking when he will come home. Karan deletes Nisha's contact and walks out of the office.

# 19. THE HEIR

During the insurgency in Kashmir in the year of 1995, **Sameer Naqvi**, a doctor based in Srinagar, agreed to perform an appendectomy on **Yaseer**, the leader of a terrorist group. To avoid being caught, he performs the surgery at his house, much to the annoyance of his wife **Saira**, who questions his allegiance. The following day, during a military raid, Sameer is accused of harbouring terrorists. A shootout ensues at his home, killing Yaseer, and Sameer is taken into custody. The doctor's house is subsequently bombed to kill any other terrorists hiding inside.

Sometime later, **Saira**'s son **Ayaan** returns after completing his education at Aligarh Muslim University to seek answers about his father's disappearance. Upon arrival, he is shocked to find his mother singing and laughing along with Sameer's younger brother, **Farhan**. Unable to understand Saira's behaviour, he begins searching for Sameer in various police stations and detention camps with the help of his childhood sweetheart **Zara**, a journalist, whose father, **Imran**, is a police officer.

Ayaan begins to lose hope as he is unable to find his father. Meanwhile, Saira and Farhan were getting closer by the day. However, Zara encounters a stranger, **Rahim**. He tells her he can help find Ayaan's father. Rahim, who is part of a pro-separatist group, explains that he and Sameer were both imprisoned in a detention camp by a counterinsurgency militia formed by Farhan. The group had both Sameer and Rahim executed, but Rahim survived. He wants to meet Ayaan to pass on Sameer's final wish. Sameer wanted Ayaan to take revenge on Farhan for his betrayal.

Devastated and enraged, Ayaan begins behaving erratically, shaving his head and staging public demonstrations against the government and AFSPA. Farhan takes him aside and claims that Rahim was responsible for Sameer's death; Ayaan is put off by the conflicting claims of Sameer's demise despite knowing the truth himself and confides his dilemma to Zara. He shows her the gun given to him to kill Farhan. Zara, in turn, confides about Ayaan's actions to Imran, her father, who in turn passes the information forward to Farhan, who orders Ayaan institutionalised during a ceremony officiating his marriage to Saira.

The following morning, Ayaan prepares to kill Farhan but morally abstains from it seeing that Farhan is in prayer. He is captured by Imran, who orders him executed. However, Ayaan escapes and brutally murders his two captors, the Salmans, former friends of his who became informants for Imran while he was away. He contacts Rahim, who suggests that he travel to Pakistan to receive military training. Ayaan calls Saira to inform her that he is going across the border, but Saira meets with him before he leaves at the ruins of their family home. She admits informing Farhan about the presence of terrorists in her home on the day of Sameer's arrest but claims to have been unaware at the time that Farhan was Imran's informant. Imran receives word of Ayaan's whereabouts and arrives at the house to assassinate him, but Ayaan kills him first and escapes.

Zara is traumatised by her father's death at the hands of her lover and commits suicide. Meanwhile, Saira finds Rahim's contact number in Zara's diary and calls him. Ayaan goes to his pickup point, the graveyard where Sameer was buried. However, he spots a nearby funeral, which he realises is for Zara. He defies the advice of his handlers and interrupts the procession, leading to a fight with Zara's brother, **Saqib**, who dies in the scuffle.

Farhan and his men arrive at the house, engaging in a gunfight that leaves most of Farhan's men dead. Saira is dropped off at the house by Rahim and begs Farhan for a chance to get Ayaan to surrender. Ayaan remains insistent on revenge, but Saira warns him that revenge merely begets revenge. She bids him farewell and returns to Farhan's men, where she detonates a suicide vest given to her by Rahim. Farhan is gravely injured and his men are killed; Ayaan prepares to kill him but remembers Saira's parting words discouraging revenge. He walks away from the site of the blast, despite Farhan's pleas to end his life.

# 20. THE ATTACK

In September 2009, the FBI arrested Rehan Siddiqui, a young Muslim man originally from Delhi, after finding guns in the trunk of a cab he owned. Rehan is then taken into custody and interrogated by FBI Agent Imran, also a Muslim man originally from Southeast Asia who has been living in the United States for the past twenty years. Imran wants to know everything about Rehan, especially his link with Faris Sheikh. Rehan then discovers that he was set up by the FBI to force him to spy on Faris, a former college friend whom he has not seen in seven years. The FBI believed he was a terrorist. In the process, Rehan discovers that Faris has married Alina, a mutual friend whom Rehan had a crush on in university and finds out that they have a young son, named Ayaan.

Imran orders Rehan to reveal everything he knows about Faris. Rehan begins his story by recounting the events of September 1999, when he started his studies at New York State University. He is befriended by his international student counsellor, Alina, and learns that though she was born and raised in New York, she is fluent in Hindi because of her mother's interest in Bollywood films. Rehan also meets and befriends Faris, an American Muslim who is not only well-spoken but also good at sports and academics. He too spoke good Hindi because his father was a professor of Indian Studies in the United States. Over the next two years, all three become inseparable friends, and gradually Rehan falls in love with Alina. When Rehan realises that she and Faris are in love, he distances himself from both of them. Their carefree days ended in September 2011 after the attacks.

After finishing his story, Rehan agrees to help Imran (rather reluctantly), because he wants to prove that both he and Faris are innocent. He reunites with Alina and Faris, who is now an architect. Rehan stays in their house, all the while spying for the FBI. He discovers that Alina is a civil rights activist who is assisting one of Faris's employees, Rafiq, in overcoming trauma as a former 9/11 detainee. Rafiq was eventually released due to a lack of evidence and has been having difficulty adjusting back to normal life.

As time passes, Rehan feels reassured that there is nothing to support the FBI's suspicions. When he hints to Faris that he might want to be a terrorist, Faris responds in a way that suggests he desires a peaceful life. However, when Rehan is ready to leave, a series of events forces him to reconsider as he meets the same suspected convicts Imran had mentioned to him earlier. Rehan is even ordered by Faris to shoot one of them for betrayal, which he reluctantly does. In the process, Rehan learns from Faris that ten days after 9/11, when he was on the way to meet Alina, he was arrested and detained for nine months at the Guantanamo Bay prison as a suspected terrorist simply because he took pictures of the twin towers for an architecture paper he was working on for his university course, weeks before the attacks and had purchased a ticket for his cousin at a Kiosk at Kinkos. This charge was eventually considered baseless by everyone, including the FBI and Imran. Though he was eventually released due to lack of evidence, the impact of being detained and tortured permanently changed Faris in ways that are difficult for those surrounding him to understand. He became more mellow and sombre and harboured deep resentment and hatred towards the FBI. He believed he was within his rights to assassinate FBI officers. Rehan thus finds that Faris ultimately resorted to terrorism as a means of revenge. Faris wanted to tell Alina about his terrorism plans but was unable to do so because she was pregnant with his child.

Once, a routine traffic stop escalates and an NYPD police officer gives Alina a very rough full-body search, agitating Rafiq. He drops Alina back home and kills the police officer the same night. After being declared a fugitive, Rafiq leads the police on a long chase ultimately ending in his suicide.

When Faris comes to know of Rafiq's death, he cancels his attack and instead decides to work on a new building contract with his sleeper cell employees, including Rehan. Meanwhile, Alina sees Rehan with Imran and discovers that he is with the FBI and might hurt Faris. She tells him that she knows about Faris. Rehan tells her that Faris has cancelled the attack and suggests that if they can provide the FBI with a guarantee assuring Faris's safety, he might abandon terrorism. However, before such a guarantee can be issued, Imran and the FBI request a meeting with Alina.

When Alina meets Imran in the FBI building, Faris, Rehan, and Faris's employees start their cleaning work. While Rehan and Adil, another of his close American-Muslim friends, are in the drainage pipes, Adil accidentally drops something from the pipe brushes, and Rehan discovers it to be the same phone bomb that Faris showed everyone, suggesting that Faris had never cancelled the terrorist attack. Rehan kills Adil, gets out of the drainage, and informs Imran that Faris is about to bomb the FBI building.

Alina, Rehan, and Imran try to prevent Faris from committing an act of terrorism by telling him that if he perpetuates terrorism, others will suffer as he has. Finally convinced, Faris surrenders and aborts his attempt to bomb the FBI building. However, the moment he drops his cell phone (which was originally intended as a detonator for the bomb), he is shot and killed by FBI snipers. The cell phone falls to the ground without activating anything. Alina, who was running towards Faris in grief, is also killed by stray gunfire, and Rehan, bereft of speech, breaks down.

Six months later, Rehan adopts Ayaan, and Imran receives a commendation for aiding in the anti-terrorism cause. Rehan is comforted by Imran, who explains to him that everybody is right in their place, but the timing is wrong. As for Faris, the path he chose killed him. Imran explains to Rehan that both Faris and Alina will always be alive in Rehan's good memories and his heart. Their friendship will always be alive because of the good times that they had spent together.

# 21. THE JUSTICE

Arvind, a superintendent of police in the Thane district, is a renowned encounter specialist known as "Thunder". He is known for taking down criminals with the help of his team and "David" Francis, a Horlicks-loving former thief-turned-police informer who also happens to be a tech genius. Arvind receives a complaint from Indu, a middle-school teacher, from Mira Bhayandar about marijuana being stored in classrooms, leading to student drug abuse and disrupted classes. Following the tip, Arvind and his team arrest Rakesh Chauhan, the man behind the drug production, and kill him in an encounter, earning public approval but drawing the scrutiny of the Human Rights Commission. Justice Rajendra attends the encounter case hearing as an observer, while the court rules the encounter justified. Indu grows closer to Arvind's family but is soon transferred to Mumbai. Indu is brutally murdered on the terrace of her new school in Mumbai, and her body is discovered in the water tank of the school. SP Sandeep Kumar and ASP Anjali Rao lead the investigation. They uncover Rohit, a software engineer and sibling of Indu's school student Sneha, as the perpetrator. Teachers protest statewide, demanding Rohit's arrest and justice for Indu. Rohit escapes custody from the hospital, prompting authorities to deploy Arvind, and is eventually tracked down and killed by Arvind in an encounter at the Bandra-Worli Sea Link. While the public praises this, Justice Rajendra reveals that Rohit was in Bengaluru at the time when the crime was committed, thus proving his innocence. Devastated by his mistake, Arvind reopens the case with David, Anjali, and Sandeep, uncovering the gaps in the original investigation. Their efforts lead them to Mahesh Patil, a contract killer, who was hired to murder Indu. However, Mahesh is killed before they discover who hired him. With David's technical expertise, the team uncovers Sandeep's corruption; he had tipped off Mahesh about the police's pursuit. Investigations with Pallavi, a Dev Academy employee, revealed their Chairman Girish Mehta's scam of luring parents and students with promises of 100% pass rates in competitive exams through online courses. Many families took loans to join, but Dev Academy refused refunds when they discontinued or could not pay; those who complained faced threats and violence. To hide the scam, Girish partnered with the government under the "Smart Student Scheme" to provide free entrance exam coaching to government schools, deceiving people by discrediting the standards of these schools and bribing social media influencers. Indu and Rohit, whose elder sister Prema was also a subscriber to Dev Academy's online course, had uncovered evidence of the scam before Indu's tragic demise. Arvind attempts to arrest Girish but is transferred to the Economic Offences Wing in retaliation. Subsequently, Arvind collaborates with DSP Nazeema to investigate Girish under the provisions of the BUDS Act, 2019. To gather evidence, Arvind, with the assistance of his wife, Sandhya, a social media influencer, collects complaints from parents across the state who claimed to have been defrauded by Dev Academy's online courses. Girish sends goons simultaneously to intimidate Arvind, Sandhya, and Anjali, but these attempts are unsuccessful. Arvind learns that a hard drive had already been sent by Indu and upon recovering finds proof of Girish's scams. But Girish's henchmen kill David during the investigation. Pallavi bribes the public prosecutor, Amit Jadhav, allowing Girish to evade a court case. Arvind, lacking concrete evidence linking Girish to Indu's murder, with his nephew, Vikram's help, shares Indu's final video, revealing Girish's purported scam and attempted murder, on social media. Then, he convenes a press meeting to share findings regarding Girish's scam, exposes Sandeep's role in falsely implicating Rohit, and declares Rohit's innocence. The government annuls all MoUs with Dev Academy, leading to its ban. During transportation from the Arthur Road prison to the court, Girish escapes custody and takes Anjali hostage. Arvind confronts Girish, and subdues him and his henchmen, securing Girish's arrest. Six months later, Girish is sentenced to life in prison, and Arvind steps back from his encounter-driven methods, choosing to let justice take its own course.

# 22. THE MISSION

Arjun Surendran, the head of a black operations (black-cats) commando squad in Salem, Tamil Nadu, is summoned by the police commissioner of the city, David, to bring justice to a group of masked vigilantes for the murder of a hardcore criminal, Sebastian. He was killed after being arrested and later released for aiding drug smugglers Arul and Mani in the murders of ACP Raghavendra, his foster father Venkat, and ACP Vijay Selvam from the Narcotics Department. Arjun investigates the case, puzzled by why Venkat, an ordinary man, was targeted alongside two senior NCB officers.

Arjun learns of Venkat's recent addiction to alcohol, drugs, and cigarettes, while concurrently being overprotective of his infant foster grandson, Rishi. While investigating, Arjun also learns of two missing shipping containers of drugs being hunted by Shankar, who runs a much bigger syndicate than Arul and Mani, named Vetti Vagaiyara. The other two containers were supposed to have been delivered to his cold-blooded smuggler boss, Rolex. The latter had promised to help Shankar form his own government if the drugs were delivered; if not, Shankar and his family would be killed. Arjun slowly figures out that all of Venkat's addictions were a ruse to cover up a covert operation, which he had been running.

Meanwhile, Muthu, a Public Works Department (PWD) officer, and a contractor named Raghunath plot to take the drug containers to Shankar, but the masked vigilantes arrive and kill Muthu. Arjun and his team capture John, one of the vigilantes. John reveals his family was killed for his role in leading a drugs bust at Trichy, leading him to join the vigilantes. Arjun and his team realise Raghunath is the vigilantes' next target, and they sneak into Raghunath's daughter's wedding ceremony. Raghunath invites Shankar for protection. The masked men and his gang arrive at the wedding and threaten him. The leader drags Raghunath and escapes on a bike, leaving the other members to deal with Shankar, who defeats them.

Arjun chases and catches the vigilante leader, who is revealed to be Venkat, who had faked his own death. However, Venkat dodges Arjun and kills Raghunath by slitting his throat and escapes the police. Arjun tells David that Venkat is actually Vikram, the former commander of the black ops squad's pilot batch of 1986. After a botched mission, the government of the neighbouring and rival country, Pakistan, hunted and killed all of the squad members and their families; only Vikram and three other team members survived. Arjun also theorises that David is Shankar's mole in the department and was involved in Raghavendra's death. After this, Arjun organises a bomb blast at Shankar's bungalow that destroys it and a drug lab. David hears of the bombing and informs Shankar. Everyone except Shankar's brother Elango is evacuated from the blast site in time. David tells Shankar about Vikram's and Arjun's identities.

Vikram arrives at the prison and frees John and his team, who were arrested and locked in different prisons by Arjun so that there is no communication between them. Vikram says the reason for his actions is not vengeance over Raghavendra's death but a mission to bust the drug syndicate in the city. Vikram also says Raghavendra is his own biological son and that Raghavendra was aware of Vikram's true identity. Shankar kills Arjun's wife, Gayathri, and sends his men to kill Vikram's wife, Lakshmi, daughter-in-law, Gauthami, and grandson, Rishi at Raghavendra's house. Vikram rushes to save them but Agent Sneha, a recently-appointed member and a recruit of Vikram's black-ops squad who was disguised as the house help Valliammal, at Shankar's residence, kills the gang at the cost of her own life, dying in the process. A vengeful Arjun kills David. Vikram and his grandson, Rishi, reach Chennai Port, where the hidden drug containers are stored. Shankar learns about the containers' location and attacks Vikram. Vikram mows down Shankar's men with a cannon and an M2 Browning, but the remaining members of his black-ops squad, who have been with him since 1986, Agents Uppiliappan, Rajagopal, and Joseph, died in the scuffle. After a fistfight with Shankar, Vikram triggers a huge blast at the port that kills Shankar and destroys the drug containers.

Sometime later, Arul and Mani arrive with their men at Sassoon Docks, Mumbai, and meet with the gangsters affiliated with Shankar, also resulting in a meeting with Rolex. Arul and Mani explain about Dhruv, the main supplier of drugs from the northern part of the country and his involvement in the recent Trichy drug ambush, and Shankar's men reveal Vikram's and Arjun's involvement in the destruction of their drug syndicate. Arjun joins Vikram's gang to continue building a drug-free society after Gayathri's funeral in Ernakulam. Mani informs Rolex that Dhruv has become more powerful than them and is hiding somewhere in Uttar Pradesh, and is nurturing a dream of overpowering both Arul and Mani, and gaining total control of the drug syndicate in Mumbai and the southern part of the country, while Shankar's men tell Rolex that Vikram's family (wife: Lakshmi, daughter-in-law,

Gauthami, and grandson, Rishi) is abroad (mentioning and describing it to be in San Francisco, USA). Rolex announces a massive bounty for the execution of Arjun, Dhruv, and Vikram's team. Unknown to everyone else, Vikram is present at the meeting in disguise and walks away with much more determination and courage after learning about the bounty placed on all three of them.

# 23. THE TRADITION

According to an ancient myth, the sting of a scorpion in Jaisalmer, Rajasthan can cause death in less than 24 hours, and the only cure is the song sung by a scorpion singer, which counters the poison of the scorpion.

Saira is an independent young woman living in a far-flung, traditional village in the desert in western Rajasthan. She comes from a tribe of scorpion singers and works as one, i.e., she heals scorpion stings by singing the song of scorpions. Saira is a beginner, yet she does not hesitate to take up cases because it is a source of income for her. The villagers disapprove of her because of her independence and shrewdness. Even Saira's grandmother, Sakina, an expert scorpion singer, rebukes her and tells her that she won't ever accept the money Saira earns by swindling poor people. Saira cannot disappoint Sakina as she loves her grandmother very much and she is the only one she has in the world. Saira keeps some money from her hard-earned income and gives the rest to her friend, Fatima, to donate to the local dargah in the village.

On one of her outings, Saira catches the eye of a camel trader named Tariq. Tariq falls instantly in love with Saira and proposes marriage to Saira, who does not respond. Tariq is thrashed by the men of Saira's village as he tries to outrage the modesty of one of their women. Saira later confides in Fatima about Tariq, but it is not clear if she has feelings for him or not.

One night, Saira gets a call from a tribesman residing in Tariq's colony, informing her about Tariq's young accomplice, Feroz, who has been bitten by a scorpion. Sakina is hesitant about sending Saira alone in the night, but Saira accepts the task. Upon reaching Feroz, Saira realises that it was a trap. Feroz tries to molest Saira and attacks her. Saira tries to run away but is only able to do so after Feroz has molested her.

In the morning, Fatima brings a wounded and traumatised Saira back home from an abandoned house in Feroz's colony, where she was hiding for most of the night, to save herself from Feroz, who had attacked and molested her. After returning to her home, Saira gets another shock. Sakina is missing. Saira looks for her grandmother everywhere, but Sakina is nowhere to be found. Out of grief and despair, Saira locks herself in the house. When Fatima comes to check on Saira, she finds some young men outside the house, passing lewd comments on Saira.

The villagers decide that Saira should be sent out of the village as she has brought a bad name upon them. The women openly suggest that Saira should go to a city and continue doing there what she's done in the village, i.e., earn her livelihood by curing people through her half-learned skill or by selling herself. With Fatima by her side, Saira resists, but both friends know that nothing is in their hands.

Her helplessness drives Saira to accept Tariq's marriage proposal. It is only when Saira moves to Tariq's house after marriage that she comes to know that Tariq is already married to Khushboo and is a father to a teenage daughter, Ayesha. Reluctantly, Saira tries to adjust to her new circumstances and becomes a friend to Ayesha.

Meanwhile, on a bright sunny day morning, Saira's grandmother, Sakina, returns home some three to four days after Saira's marriage to Tariq. When the villagers and Fatima ask her about her disappearance from her home, she tells everybody present there that on that fateful night, when Saira had gone to treat Feroz, she heard a knock on her door. Some three to four hours after Saira left, she thought that Saira had returned and opened the door at around 03:50 am. But as she opened the door, four to five masked men entered the house, hit an iron rod on her head, and made her unconscious. Then they blindfolded her and took her along with them in a jeep. She was locked in a dark room for around 10 days and was only given food for survival. During all this time, she was kept blindfolded as she would not be able to see and identify her kidnappers. After approximately 10 days, she was brought back in the same jeep and left at the corner of the road where her house was situated. So, Sakina tells everyone that she could not understand who was behind her kidnapping and her sudden release, and for what purpose she was kidnapped. Everybody, including Fatima, expresses sympathy with Sakina, but nobody could guess for what purpose the old lady was kidnapped and then released, and who was behind all that. The villagers, after hearing Sakina's story, leave for their houses. Fatima, who was also among the listeners, goes to Saira at Tariq's house and informs her about Sakina's return and her story of being kidnapped and then being released. Like others, Saira too was shocked to hear about what had happened with her grandmother, Sakina.

One night, after an altercation, Tariq releases a scorpion upon Feroz. Feroz, bitten by the scorpion and in agony, asks Tariq why he did so when he carried out everything that Tariq asked him to do, implying that Feroz had molested Saira upon Tariq's instructions so that Saira is left with no option but to accept his proposal of marrying him and that Sakina's disappearance too was orchestrated by none other than Tariq himself, to put more pressure on Saira to marry him.

A dying Feroz comes to Saira and reveals everything to her. After hearing the entire truth, Saira is shocked, and before she can do anything to save Feroz, he passes away, and Saira is unable to save Feroz. She buries his dead body in the sand outside Tariq's house.

Soon after this, Saira is revealed to be pregnant. While the female relatives celebrate, Saira is miserable. It is not clear to her if the child she is carrying is Feroz's or Tariq's.

Tariq returns home one day to find Saira missing. He goes looking for her in the dunes and finds that Saira has let one of her pet scorpions bite her. When Tariq finds Saira, she accuses Tariq of all the wrongs that he has done to her, to which a regretful Tariq tells Saira that he truly and deeply loves her and asks for forgiveness for all the miseries he has incurred upon Saira before letting one of Saira's scorpions bite him. It is then that Saira starts singing a song of scorpions, but it could not be known whether that song was meant to save herself, Tariq, or both of them. Finally, after the song ends, both Saira and Tariq are cured and saved. After this incident, both of them lived happily ever after.

# 24. THE AMBITIONS

Somewhere in Mumbai, Sameer Mehta, who is eager to move up the ranks in his call centre job, lends his apartment to people connected to his boss, Vikram Patil, for bringing their girlfriends and affair interests in turn for a recommendation. He silently loves Pooja Joshi, his colleague, who has risen in the ranks easily due to her relationship with Vikram.

Vikram is very unhappy with his marriage to his wife Anita Sharma, with whom he has an eight-year-old daughter, Avni, as he doubts her of infidelity. Anita, who often meets her aunt, Madhu Tiwari, a famous and renowned Bharatanatyam dancer, in her Bharatanatyam classes, is a frequent visitor there. One day, Madhu reads out a letter from the US from one Amol Jindal, whom Madhu loved 40 years ago, but he left her to pursue his dreams in the US. Amol conveys through the letter that he is probably coming to India for the last time and wishes to meet Madhu and spend his last days with her. Madhu agrees to Amol's demand.

Anita's sister, Kavya Sharma, is 29 and very eager to get married. She meets many prospective grooms. Among them, one is Manav Malhotra, whom Kavya finds very weird and old. Kavya is Pooja's roommate, and Pooja knows that Kavya is Vikram's sister-in-law.

One day, Anita meets Karan Kindre, an unsuccessful theatre artiste and a divorcee at a bus stop. He practices drama with his friends on the floor above Madhu's Bharatanatyam classes. They start as friends but slowly start getting close and visit places together, although non-romantically.

Manav helps Kavya get a job in his company, and they become friends. Manav also conveys that his parents, Mr Surendra Malhotra and Mrs Kusum Malhotra, have found an ideal bride for him, named Disha Chopra, and asked Kavya's help with the wedding shopping. Kavya slowly starts falling for Manav.

Amol and Madhu, who have rekindled their love, spend one night together. In the morning, Madhu, who suffers from a heart ailment due to her advancing age, wakes up and experiences some pains in her chest, at which point Amol calls for an ambulance. However, despite calling for the ambulance, Madhu cannot be saved as she suffers from a massive heart attack, and she finally dies in Amol's arms.

During one of the meetings of Pooja and Vikram in Sameer's apartment, an argument ensues between the two, and Vikram leaves. Pooja, upset, attempts suicide by drinking phenyl.

Sameer finds Pooja passed out in the bathroom and calls his neighbour, Mr Ramesh Tripathi, who, by good luck, is a doctor; thus, they can save Pooja in time by making her vomit and admitting her to a hospital. Sameer calls up Vikram, who has left for Bangalore due to an urgent business and tells him to take care of Pooja for a few days.

Sameer, meanwhile, starts taking care of the recovering Pooja, and they form a special bond. One day, Sameer takes her to the outskirts of the city to an unfinished house. Sameer explains to Pooja that his father, Mr Avinash Mehta's dream was to build a good house or a restaurant, and he had invested everything into this house. But he didn't have enough money to complete the ceiling and a few parts of the house. Now, Sameer is determined to fulfil his father's dream once again.

Kavya manages to track down Pooja in Sameer's house. Realising that she has attempted suicide, Kavya misunderstands the situation and slaps Sameer. Afterwards, Kavya finds that Vikram is having an affair with Pooja.

Meanwhile, Anita visits Karan in his home, where they get physically close. Just before they get even more intimate, Anita realises her boundaries and leaves Karan's home.

Vikram, who has arrived home, sees Anita crying and misunderstands that Kavya has told Anita about Vikram's affair. Vikram then confesses to Anita. After confessing, Anita says that Kavya never told her anything and confesses her friendship and closeness with Karan. Vikram, enraged, decides to move in with Pooja. Manav announces his wedding date to Kavya, who has fallen for him. Sameer, upset with the way the city has treated him, decides to leave Mumbai by train.

On the day of Manav's wedding, Sameer decides to leave, Vikram decides to move in with Pooja, and Karan sends Anita her handbag, which she left in Karan's house. He also sends her a letter that says he is ready to accept her the way she is: as a housewife or as a modern girl. He also writes that he has been offered a job in Dubai and is ready to leave for the airport by train, and she must come with him.

While travelling with Vikram, Pooja realises that she loves Sameer and starts chasing his taxi to the railway station. Kavya conveys her feelings to Manav right before the wedding and leaves. Manav also realises that he loves Kavya and not Disha Chopra, with whom his marriage has been fixed by his parents, and chases Kavya's taxi to the same railway station on the wedding horse. Anita dresses up and goes to the railway station.

At the railway station, Manav chases Kavya, Pooja chases Sameer, and Anita searches for Karan. Pooja catches up with Sameer, and they patch things up. Manav finally finds Kavya in a ladies' compartment and enters it. They realise their love for each other and hug. Anita finds Karan but tells him that she is not going to come with him, wishes him the best for his job in Dubai, and leaves.

The story ends after a three-and-a-half-year leap with Sameer and Pooja eating dinner with the same doctor, Dr Ramesh Tripathi, who had earlier saved Pooja's life, and his wife, Mrs Nirmala Tripathi. From their neighbourhood, Anita and Vikram are in a happier marriage, Kavya and Manav, who have married, are waiting at a traffic signal in their car with their three-year-old child, Sonu. Karan, after returning from completing his job in Dubai for two years, is still roaming the streets of Mumbai, looking to find true love once more.

# 25. THE OPERATION

Somewhere in New Delhi, RAW Agent Major **Arman Qureshi** is given the task of eliminating Al-Qaeda member, Raza Khan, and his fellow jihadis, who plan to attack New York City. The attack is being planned by Al-Qaeda on the lines similar to the 9/11 attacks of the year 2001.

Arman and his team travel to the United Kingdom to perform the final rites of one of their colleagues, John Dawkins, an Interpol officer working for Arman and his team, who was killed in a terrorist attack while supporting and assisting Arman in his home country of the United Kingdom (UK). Ananya, Arman's wife, gets jealous of Simran's (a co-officer of Arman in his many missions) closeness with Arman and asks him about the relationship between them.

Arman recalls his days in the Indian Army where he found a young, enthusiastic, brave, and highly competent lady officer, Simran, in a parade and an award ceremony. Arman and his senior Colonel Vikram together finalise Simran for their future projects, and she is trained by Arman himself. Arman was chosen for this current mission as he is the illegitimate son of a **Pakistani**, Zubair Qasim, and his mother, Devika Gupta, is an Indian. To fool his enemies for this mission, Arman and Simran created an impression that she was having an affair with Arman. He was court-martialed from the army for 10 years for being romantically involved with Simran and subsequently failing to do his duties. Arman was imprisoned but somehow managed to escape with the help of Vikram.

He was stamped as a wanted militant, and he along with his companion, Lieutenant Roy aka Imtiaz (mission name), is set for their mission to join Omar's group as fellow militants to avenge the Indian Army and the government for Arman's court-martial.

In the present, Arman, Ananya, Simran, and Vikram are well-received by Rawat, their fellow army officer, who is posted in Karachi. They arrive in Karachi, under the instructions of his superior, Raghavan. On their way in the car to hand over Dawkins's mortal remains to his family, they are attacked by a group of militants, and their car gets into a fatal accident. While Ananya, Simran, and Vikram are trapped in the car, Arman is thrown out. Arman and his team are tracked down by a militant named Aslam, and he engages in a duel with Arman's team to stop them from progressing any further in their mission in Karachi and subsequently kills Rawat in the process. Rawat succumbs to the accident and dies happily seeing his enemy's face, which was his wish as an army officer. He wanted to see the face of his enemy who was killing him and was responsible for his death.

Arman faints and is immersed in the images and flashbacks of his final encounter with Omar. Arman and Imtiaz work together to take down the terrorist groups of Raza in Karachi. Though Vikram trusts Arman completely, his senior officer, Amitabh, is suspicious of Arman, although he never conceals his suspicion of Arman's loyalty to India.

Arman tries to place a locator in Omar's den to give the coordinates of Al-Qaeda's prime leader, Mullah Mohammed, to the NATO troops. One day, Raza catches Arman red-handed and fires at him, but Imtiaz is killed instead. Arman escapes from Raza and signals flares for friendly choppers. However, Arman is heavily wounded in the attack. Vikram deploys the army soldiers to take him to the hospital, where he is eventually saved.

Back to the present, all the accident victims reach their hotel in Karachi, where they are well-received by Raghavan. Raghavan and Arman engage in an argument for killing the terrorists, led by Aslam, who had attacked them in an encounter by Arman and his team, instead of catching them red-handed. Raghavan taunts Arman for being a Mohammedan and doubts his loyalty towards his home country, India, but Arman says he is a proud Muslim who is willing to sacrifice his life for his country. Raghavan leaves the place angrily.

Arman and Simran scan the room for bugging devices and eventually find one, break it into pieces, and ask Raghavan not to try anything with it. Arman and Ananya get into a romantic act but are interrupted by a call for a meeting with Vikram, Raghavan, and an ISI agent, who turns out to be Munnawar. Arman suspects Raghavan's hand in the terrorist attack on them. Arman, Simran, and Ananya leave to scan a building, along with the ISI agent, Munnawar, in a place outside the city to track down the terrorist activities of Raza and his gang in the city of Karachi. Arman and Raghavan engage in a phone call during Arman's visit to the building to search for bombs, which are hidden by Raza and his gang in that building for use against India. Raghavan insists Arman leave the building, but Arman disobeys. Arman left the building but pretends to have got trapped inside the building. Raghavan triggers a bomb with the help of his cell phone and is quite happy that Arman is killed. However, Munnawar informs him that Arman is alive and has escaped the scene. Arman threatens Raghavan that he has revealed himself and he will hunt him down at any cost. Raghavan kills himself to avoid getting caught by Vikram, Arman, and their team.

The team finds a book in the building, which is showing the tide timings of the area. Inside the building, they trace a flashback showing how the US sent 1500 tons of weapons and explosives to the British aboard the famous ship **SS Richard Montgomery** on the 29th of July 1943 during the **Second World War**, but the ship sank just before reaching London on the 20th of August 1944 and the explosives on board are still there.

They figure out that Raza and his militants are trying to use these caesium weapons to blow them underwater in India to trigger the dormant explosives on the shipwreck. If done during high tide, this could cause an explosion so big that it would create a **tsunami** and immerse the city 10 to 16 metres below sea level. The team plans to fly and hurry to **Sheerness**, the town where the shipwreck is located, to reach there before Raza and his militants can deactivate these weapons and bombs. After reaching **Sheerness**, Ananya, who owns a deep-sea diving certificate, dives underwater to examine the caesium weapons and tries to deactivate them.

However, before Arman and his team can fulfil their mission, they are attacked by Shahadat, an aide of Omar, and in this attack, Arman's acquaintance and a team member, Jim, are killed by Shahadat and his militants. Soon, Arman learnt that Shahadat and his team were planning to attack his team and use AI-generated mechanisms to track them down before they could inflict further damage on Arman and his team. Shahadat and his men try to remotely blast the bombs underwater to kill

Ananya, who has dived underwater to examine and deactivate the weapons. Arman kills all of them, including Shahadat, before they can kill Ananya.

The team reaches New Delhi, and Vikram is called alone by his senior, Amitabh for debriefing. Arman, Ananya, and Simran reach their previously booked rooms in New Delhi to have a rest. Seeing Simran and Arman sleeping in the same bed, Ananya gets angry. She leaves for a nearby coffee shop, where she overhears Vikram's debriefing session with his senior Amitabh. Vikram and Amitabh argue about Ananya's role in the team. Amitabh asks him to get rid of her, but Vikram refuses as Arman loves her more than anything and they have to respect his feelings. Ananya is moved by Arman's love for her. She returns to him, and the two make love, while Simran has moved to her room. Ananya and Arman later go to meet Arman's mother, Mrs Devika Gupta, who is an Alzheimer's patient, living in a care home in New Delhi. Arman's mother could not recognise her son but is always lamenting looking at the childhood photos of her son. He recalls the days when she used to lead the Kathak sessions, back when she was younger and in good health, with Arman assisting her during those sessions.

The very next day, Simran and Ananya are kidnapped by Farhan, Omar's right-hand man, from their respective rooms in the hotel. Simran tries to knock him down, but he breaks her forearm, brutally dismembering her hand from her body. After keeping her hostage for three days, he kills her and sends her chopped body to Arman. Arman, on the other hand, has been desperately looking for Simran and Ananya for the past three days. Upon receiving Simran's mutilated body and the information about Ananya, Arman is devastated and curses himself for not being able to save them. Arman finally packs his bags and decides to go alone to Omar's den in Karachi, where Farhan has held Ananya as a hostage.

Arman arrives in Karachi and, after locating Omar's den with the help of GPS and AI techniques, heads straight to Omar's den. As soon as he reaches Omar's den, he finds Ananya imprisoned with her hands behind her back in handcuffs as Omar's hostage. Arman begs Raza to spare Ananya, but Raza refuses, saying that Arman was the reason behind the death of his family members during the NATO attack. He states he will not leave Ananya and will kill her to avenge the death of his family members.

Arman tells Raza that his wife, sons, and nephew are alive. He explains that he handed them over to NATO to be taken to a safe haven, not to be killed. Omar, after listening to Arman, says he does not believe him and insists on killing Arman. However, after listening to Arman, he pretends to spare Ananya.

Ananya is then taken to **Daryaganj**, an outskirt of New Delhi, where Arman's mother too has been kidnapped by Omar's New Delhi module and kept as a hostage. After Farhan informs Raza that they have reached their **Daryaganj** hideout, Arman, who is now handcuffed by Omar's men, gets a bomb planted around his neck by Omar's assistants with a 40-second timer.

Farhan then tells Ananya about their master plan to celebrate 77 years of Indian Independence. They have planted 77 bombs in and around the city of New Delhi, which will be detonated by an **SMS** on the 15th of August. Arman tries to free himself from the clutches of Omar's assistants. With half of the timer elapsed, Arman manages to free himself from the shackles placed by Omar's assistants. He throws the time bomb at them before escaping from Omar's den by jumping out of a window, smashing the glass pane, and narrowly avoiding the bomb. Before Raza and his men could understand what had happened, Arman had already escaped from their den. Just then, when Omar's gang understands the situation, the time bomb explodes, leaving most of the gang members dead and many others, including Raza himself, badly burnt from the blast of the time bomb.

On the other hand, in **Daryaganj**, New Delhi, Farhan and his men see the bomb blast, which was triggered in Karachi by Arman, killing many gang members of Raza and leaving Raza himself badly burnt. This leaves Farhan and his men totally dejected and in a fit of rage. After witnessing the Karachi incident, Farhan, along with his men, attacked Ananya. However, when Farhan and his men were watching the Karachi blast live on television, Ananya freed her hands from the handcuffs and counter-attacked Farhan and his men.

Before Farhan tries to gun Ananya down, she grabs a machine gun lying on the floor and shoots Farhan and all his men dead. After killing Farhan and all his men, Ananya gets hold of the plan the terrorists had made for the 15th of August and takes the entire blueprint with her. Before leaving Farhan's den, she sets the entire hideout on fire, resulting in a massive explosion as Farhan's hideout is full of explosives. After emerging from Farhan's den, which is now a heap of debris, Ananya immediately leaves for Karachi on the first flight available to meet Arman and inform him about the terrorists' plans for the 15th of August.

Upon arriving in Karachi, Ananya and Arman reunite, and Ananya hands over the entire blueprint of the terrorists' plot to bomb New Delhi with 77 bombs, which she had gathered from Farhan's Daryaganj den. Arman sends the entire blueprints to his headquarters in New Delhi to his boss, Vikram, as well as to his superior, Amitabh. Vikram and Amitabh arrange for the deactivation of all the bombs, which the bomb squad deactivates, thus saving New Delhi from the grave danger of a big terrorist attack. After the bombs are deactivated, Vikram and Amitabh congratulate Arman and Ananya for foiling the terrorists' plot and saving New Delhi from a big danger, as well as killing most of the terrorists associated with this terror plot. Arman and Ananya rejoice in Karachi over the success of their mission, as do the entire RAW team members based in the city of New Delhi.

After the success of their mission, Arman and Ananya visit the hospital in Karachi, where Raza is admitted in a very bad condition with over 90 per cent burns. Arman enters Omar's ward and shows Omar's sons to Omar, stating that Jalaal (the elder son) has finished his engineering and is moving to London for his MTech and Nasser (the younger son) is in his first year of medical college at a top medical college in New York. Arman also tells him that his wife, Zahida, and his nephew, Imraan, are also safe and sound and far from the dangerous world of terrorism. Arman informs Raza that his sons will not become terrorists in the future and that his family members are far away from the bloody world of terrorism and insurgency.

Omar, on his deathbed, realises his mistake and thanks Arman for saving both his sons, as well as his wife and nephew, and keeping them away from the fatal world of terrorism and militancy, and dies peacefully. Arman, along with Ananya, quietly walks out of the hospital, relieved and satisfied that their operation is finally complete and successful. They are relieved that India is safe from the terrorist attack planned for its 77th Independence Day and that all the terrorists responsible have been eliminated.